THE HEIST ARTIST

Vish Dhamija is the bestselling author of seven crime fiction books. He is frequently referred to in the press as the 'master of crime and courtroom drama' in India. In August 2015, at the release of his first legal fiction, *Deja Karma*, *Glimpse* magazine called him, 'India's John Grisham' for stimulating the genre of legal fiction in India, which was almost non-existent before his arrival on the scene. *The Heist Artist* is his eighth novel. Vish lives in London with his wife, Nidhi.

VISH
DHAMIJA

THE
HEIST ARTIST

HARPER
BLACK
An Imprint of HarperCollins *Publishers*

First published in India in 2019 by Harper Black
An imprint of HarperCollins *Publishers*

Building 10, Tower A, 4th Floor, DLF Cyber City, Phase II,
Gurugram Haryana – 122002, India
www.harpercollins.co.in
2 4 6 8 10 9 7 5 3 1

P-ISBN: 978-93-5302-602-8
E-ISBN: 978-93-5302-603-5

Typeset in 11/14 Bembo at
Manipal Digital Systems, Manipal

Printed and bound at
MicroPrints India, New Delhi

MAP ONE

The Route from Barakhamba Road, New Delhi to Bhimdatta in Far-Western Nepal.

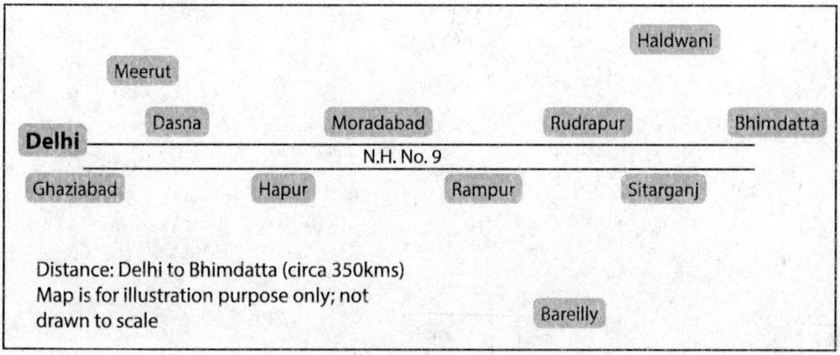

MAP TWO

Main towns/cities where a large part of the action in the book takes place.

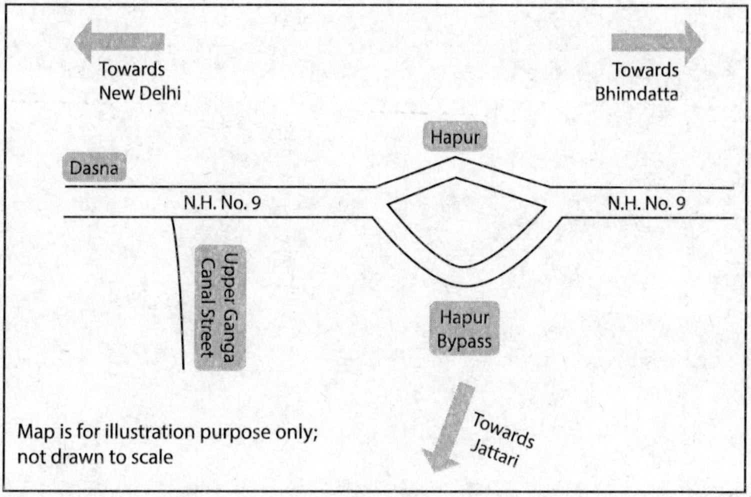

The event: The Third Prudential Cricket World Cup

Venue: Lords, London

Date: 25 June 1983

Teams: India vs West Indies

The favourites: West Indies

The underdogs: India

London bookies were offering 66:1 odds against India. In one word – hopeless. But it also meant that if you played those desperate odds and wagered one lakh rupees on the Indian Team on that morning of 25 June 1983, you would have made sixty-six lakh rupees by the evening.

Desperate odds deter most people because the outcome of any event is so blatantly obvious. And most people like to play safe. Why should any sound person gamble on a losing horse?

Well, what most people fail to grasp is that the outcome is only *almost* obvious, never definitive.

Remember, some people had still bet on those desperate, hopeless odds of 66:1.

Sometimes people play those odds because they have nothing left to lose.

From the Delhi Police files:

Name: Vagh Pratap Singh aka 'Captain'. Photograph and fingerprints on file.

Three arrests. One trial. No convictions.

Charges: Suspected of armed robbery and complicity in manslaughter besides several break-ins, thefts, frauds and forgeries.

Physical description: 5'11", eighty-five/ninety kilograms. Real eye colour: chocolate brown, but uses coloured lenses. Sometimes wears glasses: clear or coloured, big or small. Hair colour: dark brown, but frequently changes to salt-pepper, white, wigs or completely shaved. A 'master of disguise', he changes his appearance from handsome to intimidating or extremely charming/friendly to downright offensive/hostile.

Personality: Charming, to the extent of being hypnotic.

Expertise: Skilled at breaking into any safe, evading security cameras. May work/seek employment in enterprises like private security firms or work as doorman/bodyguard/driver or in other similar capacities that can provide him with inside knowledge or a chance to gain trust to facilitate access.

Age: 40. Divorced almost a year ago, no contact with ex-wife.

DoB: Unknown.

Background: Unknown.

Parents: Both dead.

Last known profession: Sadhu/sanyasi.

Last known guise: Dreadlocks and a long, flowing beard.

Last known location: Near Kalbhairav Temple, Benares.

Current whereabouts: Unknown.

Caution: Can be armed. Approach with extreme caution.

Call it confidence or call it my sixth sense, but I honestly believe that the Delhi Police have horseshit on me.

Or am I delusional? – The Captain

1

THE CAPTAIN'S STORY

'An amateur looks at Vincent van Gogh's 1889 work, the oil on canvas titled *Self-Portrait with Bandaged Ear,* and sees the artist's right ear bandaged. And this amateur assumes that it was his right ear the Dutch painter mutilated, because only an amateur doesn't know that Van Gogh painted his self-portraits with bandaged ear using his reflection in a mirror, and it was actually his left ear that was severed …'

'Excuse me, Mr Reuben,' a bright young lady in my class interposed. Sheena Marwah.

I have always considered this a positive sign. If nothing else, a question suggested that at least someone had been listening.

I was an Art professor in Delhi Technological University's College of Art. I had joined the department four months back, when the previous professor suddenly decided to take an early retirement during the middle of the term. Well, he didn't take the decision on his own. Someone had made him a Godfather-esque offer. Not with a gun, but with a wad of cash.

In the two months preceding my appointment in the college, I had brushed up on my knowledge of art. I covered in a month what people take years to study and probably a lifetime to accomplish. Intensity, colour, tone, rhythm. The aesthetics. The modern styles – impressionism, abstract, surrealism. Art is a vast field, almost infinite. But I made my own little cheat sheet. I was exactly like a newbie swimmer who sticks to the sides. I couldn't go mid-stream; those art sharks would discern blood from red ink instantly. And hence, I focussed on all the things I believed others might have dismissed as trivia.

My plan was to use that trivia to point out the significant misses of the art world; to use those pointless intricacies to trash the existing so-called experts by boring holes in their papers, in their impressions and theories about a particular piece of work or an artist's repertoire. Why else would I care if Vincent van Gogh sliced off his left ear or his right? It adds or takes nothing away from his paintings.

But on that day, like the last four months, what I was subliminally impressing upon my handful of students was that I was not simply another ordinary art critic or a mere professor; I went beyond what was evident to most.

Honestly, in my opinion, not many people know much about art. A lot is just hot air. There are two purported appreciators of art: wealthy collectors who buy a piece of art – painting, sculpture, sketch, whatever – solely as an investment or to get into a pissing contest with other such wealthy pseudo art lovers. 90 per cent of them couldn't distinguish oil from watercolour if their lives depended on it. They buy what they know about. How could anyone possibly go wrong by investing in a Picasso or a Monet or an MF Hussain? The other group, the real aficionados, are the artists themselves. But most living artists can't afford the works of the ones considered even remotely collectable.

Anyway, I didn't give a rat's ass about art. But I wasn't here by chance. Everything had been planned to the T. I had a new wardrobe, and had my dreadlocks cut so that my hair was now set in a slightly long, carefree style – a creative person, not a geography professor. I did look the part. And so far, no one had detected my deception. And I was confident they wouldn't. Not in the short term, anyway, and it wasn't like I was here for life. I was in the process of establishing my reputation as an Asian authority on Van Gogh for a reason.

'You have a question for me, Sheena?' I gave her a wide, practised smile. Sheena asked the most questions. She also had a penchant for digressing from art into her life, which she often attempted to portray as a wild one – a carefree soul, an art buff, married but flirtatious.

'You just said *self-portraits* with bandaged ear … did he do more than one of those?'

I was glad she had caught that. I needed this piece of my lecture to travel far and wide into their rich social circles. I had a total of eighteen students, and most of them attended all my lectures. Don't ask me why, but they were all women.

'Yes. He painted two of them in 1889. There is one that the whole world knows about, or has at least seen the picture of, and it is in Courtauld Gallery at Somerset House in London.'

'The one with the geishas in the background?'

'Correct. He painted a Japanese woodblock print alongside a canvas and easel in the background,' I carried on.

'I've seen that one, Mr Rueben. I was in London last summer with my husband. As usual, he was busy with business meetings, and so I spent my time at art galleries, museums—'

'Yes, so …' I interrupted her before she could digress further. 'Van Gogh, as you know, was inspired by Japanese art at the time, especially by Hokusai, since both artists shared a passion for portraying everyday lives of the working class. Van Gogh's second *Self-Portrait with Bandaged Ear and Pipe* has a simpler, plainer background. As the name suggests, in that he's smoking a pipe, and you can see a plume of smoke rising. It's marginally smaller, and it is in someone's private collection, but no one knows where.'

'How come?' Anita, another one of my students, asked. She was in her early thirties, married as well and a mother of one.

'Perhaps because whoever owns it doesn't want the world to know that they have it.'

'Do you think it's because they are afraid someone might steal it from them?'

A few more students sat up, clearly much more interested in the conversation now.

'That could be one of the reasons,' I agreed.

'But what would anyone *do* with a stolen painting?' asked Gayatri – young, sharp and perhaps the only real art aficionado in my class. She was also the only student in my class who was an artist herself.

'Sell it, of course!' Sheena responded before I could.

'Who'd buy a stolen painting?' Gayatri asked.

'A work of art is always sold before it's stolen,' I said.

'What do you mean?'

'I mean, it's almost certain that whoever steals such an expensive piece would have already found a buyer for it. Or more likely, the thief would have been hired by some collector to steal the piece for them. So Gayatri, in a way you're right. It's not like someone can filch a Van Gogh and put it on eBay.'

'And how many times has a Van Gogh painting been stolen?' Sheena asked.

'Several times. Van Gogh's works have been stolen several times.'

I could see that I had them hooked. The class no longer wanted to discuss Van Gogh's vertical strokes or his reluctance towards mixing colours on the palette or the story behind his masterpieces. No, now they only wanted the trivia and controversies surrounding the artist.

'One of Van Gogh's works, *Blossoming Chestnut Branches*, was stolen from Foundation E.G. Bührle gallery in 2008 but was found just nine days later in a parked car in Zurich. *The Ramparts of Paris* was stolen in Manchester in 2003, but it, too, was recovered in a matter of days.'

Their mouths were now agape; they were eating my words and swallowing them whole, digesting them.

'*Congregation Leaving the Reformed Church in Nuenen* is another work that's gone missing – this one, along with the *View of the Sea at Scheveningen*, was stolen from the Van Gogh Museum in Amsterdam in 2002. They were both recovered in 2016 in Naples.'

'So have all the stolen paintings been recovered?'

'Well, no. *Poppy Flowers,* a painting he created in 1887, three years before he committed suicide, is still missing. It was once stolen in 1978, but was recovered after a couple of years. Then, it was reported stolen again in 2010 from the Mohamed Mahmoud Khalil Museum in Giza. It hasn't resurfaced since. Gone, vanished.'

I could see them leaning forward, eating up my words. I went on. I had them exactly where I needed them.

'It's missing, but the rumour mill has been working overtime since then …'

I paused deliberately.

'What are the rumours?' someone asked eagerly, just as I'd hoped.

'Well, some people have traced the path the painting could have taken – from Cairo to Dubai to Hong Kong. It's said that it purportedly got sold for over sixty million US dollars to a private collector.'

'Is *Poppy Flowers* more coveted because of its chequered history?'

'That is one of the reasons, yes. After all, it has been stolen twice, and is still missing!' My confidence was rising. I had been preparing for this moment for months now. When I started teaching here, I couldn't have delivered this lecture so convincingly. Now they trusted me, all eighteen of my students. I could sell them a fake Van Gogh tomorrow and they'd lap it up as the real deal on my say so.

I cast my eyes across the small classroom to look at all of them, one by one. I'd heard that the word *con* comes from confidence, which is really a state of mind more than anything else. I had been at poker tables, played high odds, and I could endorse that the centuries-old adage – *you don't play the cards, you play the opponents* – was spot-on. Whoever blinked first lost.

'There are two other reasons that make this painting precious,' I continued, and saw heads nodding in anticipation.

'One – not many people across the world have seen it since it left Italy in the seventies, because Egypt wasn't on the world map for art lovers. That increases the curiosity value around it, which always hikes up the price. Secondly, some art publication once claimed in an article that *Poppy Flowers* was a personal favourite of the master himself – that can't be confirmed, of course, but you probably know that some people will believe anything they read in print.'

I could feel the interest of the room rising, becoming more intense and focussed. The questions came rapidly now.

'What size is it?'

'It's not very big; twenty-six inches by twenty-one. Oil on canvas. It's got yellow and red poppies against a dark background.'

'Where do you think it could be?'

Exactly the question I had been waiting for.

'Well … there was some serious bidding in the clandestine art world in Hong Kong, and in the end, it is rumoured to have been bought by some erstwhile Nawab from India, an art patron. The Nawab died soon after, bequeathing his prized collection to his son, who turned out to be a real loser – a classic story of riches to rags.' I stopped and smiled. 'But like I said, these are just rumours.'

'You have got to be kidding me!' Sheena exclaimed.

'The Nawab's prodigal son is said to have either pawned or sold the collection for cash, and then never managed to recover any of the paintings from it.'

'How much would *Poppy Flowers* be worth now?' asked another student.

'In 1990, *Portrait of Dr Gachet* sold for eighty-two point five million US dollars.'

'What?' A few of them shouted in unison.

'So other than the rumours, we have no real info on where *Poppy Flowers* could be now?' another student piped up.

'No. No one knows that for sure.'

Well, this wasn't exactly true. I had a shortlist of four people – two businessmen who were art collectors, a politician and an erstwhile Nawab. Four possible suspects, right here in India. But my students didn't need to know all that.

'How will the owner know if what they have is an original? Will a fake Van Gogh be easy to spot, Mr Rueben?'

'Not necessarily. Many painters can replicate a Picasso or a Rembrandt or a Van Gogh so brilliantly that a lay person can't even tell the difference.'

'So there's no way to establish if the *Poppy Flowers* that belongs to someone in our country – if it is still in India – is the original one?'

'Of course, there is,' I said. 'That can be determined by any Impressionist era expert, or by someone who specialises in Van Gogh's works,' I slipped myself in without quite saying it outright. 'There is a certain style, and then there is the age of the painting itself … But that doesn't mean that a rookie can identify a fake …'

'What, according to you, would be its value, if it was really an original?'

'The approximate value is currently put at fifty to fifty-five million US dollars, but the real value, I'd say, can go up to around 150 million US dollars. It really depends on how much interest the painting generates, and how many buyers there are.'

Once again, I was being economical with the truth. I knew the painting was worth 200 million US dollars, because it already *had* a buyer in Japan. I knew that the deal had already been made. I also knew who was selling the painting to him. *And* I could tell you who was being paid to deliver it to the seller – Professor Albert Rueben, a Vincent van Gogh expert, erstwhile Fine Arts professor at Hautes études commerciales aka HEC, Paris.

And no, I was never an arts professor at HEC. But the office clerk here in Delhi had had a motorcycle accident the day he was meant to send the mail asking for references from HEC. When the poor man returned to work, everything had already been taken care of, the references received and filed by the temporary staff. I don't need to tell you that the clerk's accident wasn't just a piece of good luck. Neither was the temporary member of staff helpful without a reason. The person who had been managing everything for me in the background wasn't doing it all for charity either.

So, there it was – the only reason for my sudden interest in Shri Vincent van Gogh.

ONE YEAR AGO

2

THE CAPTAIN'S STORY

The legend goes that once, long, long ago, some saints approached Lord Brahma to ask him if he was the supreme and eternal power. Being the creator, Lord Brahma cheerfully agreed that yes, he certainly was. When Lord Vishnu learned of this, he challenged the claim, declaring it hasty and insolent. After all, it was in fact him, Lord Vishnu, who was the Narayan and ergo, the ultimate power. The two warring gods turned to the Vedas for an answer.

Long story short, all of the four Vedas unanimously declared Lord Shiva the supreme and eternal power. He was the only one who could eliminate all the troubles of this world. When Lord Brahma didn't concede, Lord Shiva created *Kaal Bhairav* – the king of *Kaal*, the most fearsome expression of Lord Shiva himself, and ordained that this '*Kotwal* of Benares' would forever live in this shrine to absolve the sins of his disciples.

I hadn't known about the temple or its legacy before I set foot in Benares last year. But then I hadn't come to the city to take a dip in the Ganga to wash off my sins either. I hadn't sinned. Well, I might be a criminal in the eyes of the law, but that's not necessarily a sin. I came to Benares because I was sick of the law enforcements in Delhi chasing me. I had this feeling that I was constantly being followed, like they were looking for a reason to arrest me again.

I'd been to jails. A few times, in fact. But I was never convicted of anything grave enough to keep me there for long. I'd always plead guilty to some lesser charge, something innocuous, like a traffic violation. A minor sentence and a slap on the wrist, at the most. It'd help the arresting officer save face too. A win-win. I made sure they never found anything bigger against me.

But with no regular job, I had been living off petty crimes, and it was getting tiring. I call them petty crimes because my share of the loot had always been frugal. The capers, the thefts, the burglaries, the dubious deals were always organised by the biggies. Some upright businessmen, some holier-than-thou politicians, and some rank in-your-face criminals. I'd been hired, fired, and thrown into the firing line as a scapegoat.

But after my last antic, a slightly more hazardous one than my previous accomplishments, the police were hot on my trail. It had been an arms deal – a consignment of illegal weapons that were bought by a politician and needed transportation from Bahadurgarh in Haryana to Greater Noida. Merely eighty-odd kilometres, but considering the route passed through New Delhi – the capital of the country – it wasn't exactly child's play.

In retrospect, I know that someone must have tipped off the police.

I'd hot-wired a white Honda Accord at ten from an office complex in Haryana merely an hour before I had to pick up the consignment. I was positive that its owner wouldn't even miss the vehicle before the end of office hours. But even so, I had changed the car's registration plates. What if the police issued a bulletin for its search? Why take the risk? I could have picked up a smaller car, but I knew from experience that the more desperately you try to be unnoticed, the more attention you draw from trained police eyes.

All started well. I handed the cash over and picked up the heavy cricket bag with twelve virtually new pieces – ten Glock 17s and two Heckler & Koch MP5s, along with an assortment of magazines and cartridges. I had used guns before, but most of them had been those old and rusty hand-me-downs that you can't be certain will actually shoot straight or just blow up in your hand; never had I handled such shiny, nearly new pieces. Clearly, some corrupt police officer had sold them, as I had seen the same make of guns being used by the Delhi Police.

I drove out after 4 p.m. and put on the radio – music always calms my nerves. Passing the traffic infested Jahangirpuri Industrial area, I took National Highway 10 and cruised between a 100 and 105 kmph. I knew that if anyone conscientiously drove below the speed limit, they'd raise suspicion. Those clever police officers could smell when something wasn't right, like if they saw an over-cautious driver. But that didn't mean I could floor the pedal. That would certainly raise their antennas too, like I was running away from something. It's when I turned left onto the Outer Ring Road after Paschim Enclave that I noticed a white Toyota Qualis. It had come out of nowhere.

Maybe it had been parked on the side and only got on to the Ring Road after I passed it. It had its siren blaring and its red beacon lit. They were about 400 metres behind me when they started flashing their headlights. I looked in the rear-view mirror to confirm what I already knew. They were on to me. But I was in no mood to stop with twelve guns in a bag on the rear seat. I looked around to check if there were any more vehicles besides the one I could see. None. This didn't mean that there wasn't a blockade ahead, but I wasn't going to just give myself up to two khakis in a Qualis. One of my skills, because of which I continually got assignments from my hirers, was my driving proficiency. They couldn't chase me down even if they had an identical Accord; forget taking me on in a Qualis. The traffic was scant, a point in my favour, as I didn't want to cause an accident or injure an innocent person. And now that I was already being pursued, I didn't have to worry about breaking the speed limit. What would they do? Book me for speeding? I pressed the pedal and the Accord sped ahead. Intermittently looking into the rear view mirror, I saw that the passenger in the pursuing vehicle was relentlessly talking on the radio. Calling for a backup, probably. If someone had snitched on me, it was likely the police knew where I was headed. This meant there would be a second or a third vehicle, either on the way ahead or arriving at the scene soon. And they could come from any direction. The first police car might have been in place only to affirm the legitimacy of the tip. But now they knew I was bolting.

My pulse started racing. Being caught with guns meant it would be a long sentence, even if I called in all my favours. They could book me under The Prevention of Terrorism Act, 2002 (POTA), or some such thing and I'd never see the blue sky again. I pushed the car harder. The distance between my hunters and me was about 800 metres now. I knew there was a water treatment plant around seven or eight kilometres ahead. Adrenaline pumped within me. If I forged enough distance between the police and me, I could possibly slip off into the plant. I'd have to discard the car and run on foot into the vast greens of the plant and hide somewhere with the merchandise. I pulled out my Blackberry and looked at it, but it was impossible to use it with gloves on. I was content to see that it had enough juice for me to call someone later.

I raced on. The signage for Haiderpur Water Treatment Plant appeared two kilometres before the site. I was at 140, and the Qualis to be a kilometre behind me now. If it weren't for its shining beacon, it would just be a small white cube sliding towards me. There were three oversized truck-trailers ahead, which could slow me down. I moved in the right lane to appraise them. All Volvos. They all appeared to belong to the same company, carrying heavy loads to the same destination. Three of them meant a total length of circa fifty metres – add the distance between them and it totalled to eighty metres of the road. It instantaneously clicked in that I could use them as my insurance. I swerved right, overtook the first, second and then the third Volvo in a single, file and cut back left, straight in front of the third one. I heard loud honking from the rear. The driver in the leading truck had obviously not expected a car to steer back to the left just ahead of him so sharply, instead of going straight ahead. Not that he had to break speed, but still. I did that because I knew that staying in the right lane would have provided my hunters with a clear view of my car. Then I started decelerating. The police were a kilometre behind me. They were probably doing a 100-125 in the Qualis, since they had been losing ground against me in the race. A kilometre behind me at 120 per minute translated to approximately thirty seconds to cover the kilometre. Simple maths. I braked hard, slowing the Accord to let the truck-trailers behind me catch up with me, and then I veered slightly left, taking my vehicle off the tarmac. I was now at a twenty-degrees angle – half the car on the blacktop, half on the unpaved dirt. My car left a cloud of dust in the back. I counted to fifteen. My calculation told me that the police behind me should be overtaking the three trucks now. I counted to a further five, braked down to seventy and took the car totally off the tarmac, letting the three trucks behind pass me by. Then I slowed down to forty kmph. It's one of the oldest tricks in the book for a good cover-up. The large truck-trailers were on my right, but they were still in the left lane and the Qualis was going past them on their right. I'd be shielded for a minute or two till the police overtook the three trucks and gathered that I wasn't ahead of the vehicles that they had just overtaken. Plus a minute to realise what could have happened, and yet another one or two valuable minutes to spot me in the passenger-side wing mirror if they were diligent and quick. And they couldn't just jam their brakes with three large lorries following them; the Qualis would be flattened. So, add another four-five minutes before they slowed, took their vehicle off the road, did a 180 degree turn or reversed to where I was. That was a minimum of an eight minute lead for me in the worst of circumstances and definitely no more than ten at best. But eight minutes is four hundred and eighty seconds, long enough for me to get out of the car, pick the large bag, and escape on foot into the water treatment plant; it was dusk already, visibility would only get poorer.

I called a friend for a pick up at midnight, after I was confident that the police had either given up the chase or the search party had gone elsewhere.

However, I took the opportunity to pinch two handguns, both the machine guns and lots of ammunition. I reckoned it would be simple to explain that I had to dump some of the stock when I was on foot to lighten my bag, if I had to outrun the police.

I had been right. Someone had ratted out the whole operation. Later, the police did find me, but as always, they didn't find a grain of evidence. They kept me in lockup for the maximum time they could – fourteen days. Then I was released on bail. The politician I was running the errand for got me out, but he was not convinced I had actually lost the weapons. I was cajoled and threatened, but I didn't give in.

After that, I left Delhi. I was facing a lot of heat. The police, as well as the crooked politician, had started dogging me 24/7. When the law and hoodlums are both against you, any attempt at bravery is stupid – it's smarts that you need. I knew that it was time to take flight, to get out of their hair and lie low for a while.

I picked Benares.

I didn't go to Benares directly. I first travelled to Pushkar, where I let my hair and beard grow. I spent time there, picking up the sadhu jargon, mannerisms and eating habits. I had to cope without alcohol and adopt vegetarianism. I needed them to believe that I was a bona fide godman, that I belonged. Before getting to Benares, I had to belong in Pushkar.

Which wasn't too far from the truth, actually.

I was born in Ajmer. My father ran a small enterprise that specialised in block printing fabric using natural vegetable dyes. He supplied the same to a large exporter in Jaipur. I was an only child. We were a small and happy family – my mother, father and I. My father often said that, when I grew up, we would all move to Jaipur, cut out the middleman, and export directly. He wanted the best for us. I used to attend a premier school in the city. And then, everything changed.

I remember that day distinctly – that night, to be precise. We were awakened by noises in the house. Someone had broken in. We had an old early twentieth-century large, British style bungalow with a large veranda that ran all around the front, and a living and dining area that led to an open courtyard in the middle, which had bedrooms around it. The courtyard, though open to the sky, had iron bars to prevent burglars. The rooms at the front of the house had high ceilings and windows with protective grills. However, the *roshandaans* – the little ventilator windows high above the windows – had glass shutters only, and the burglar simply took the glass out of the frame from one of them and slipped in. With the ensuing noise, my father woke up, switched on the lights and saw the guy. The thief unbolted the front door and made a run for it. He hadn't had the time to take anything, and my father should have left it at that. The police complaint could have been filed the next morning; the *roshandaan* glass could have easily been replaced too. I remember my mother yelling, warning my father not to go out after the burglar – especially since we didn't know how many of them there were. Agreed, only one person had come into the house, but there could be others waiting outside. But my father was a large man – 6'2", a

110 kilos, and righteous. For him, a thief was a thief, whether the offender got away with anything or left empty-handed. He ran after the man, chased him down to the end of the street, but in the little fight that followed, the thief stabbed him twice with a long knife. My father didn't survive.

I remember our neighbours and friends and relatives pouring in over the days that followed. I remember the police doing fuck-all to catch my father's murderer – they made excuses, leered at my mother, asked her for money and left.

Being able to remember everything is a curse. Memories sometimes leave behind indelible marks that can haunt a person for a lifetime.

We had been a typical patriarchal household. My father brought in the money and my mother ran the household. Consequently, after his death, the usual despondency followed. My mother had no knowledge of my father's business. No one contacted her for the orders that were in the pipeline. The creditors – some of them allegedly my father's closest friends – started knocking on our doors even before his ashes had cooled. The business went belly up within months. My mother sold her jewellery first, and then our bungalow. I was fourteen when I had to be pulled out of the private school and sent to a government one. My mother got a job as some sort of caretaker in a primary school.

I also remember the day my mother passed away. And while her passing was not as dramatic as my father's, it was equally sad for me.

I remember leaving town at twenty-two – heartbroken and penniless.

By the time I arrived in Benares, no one would have pegged me for a novice, and no one treated me as one either. I was just another sadhu who had moved to the city to reside in the shadow of Lord Shiva. To work for other men, you need prior experience and references, but to work for God, you need nothing. No one checked back at Pushkar to see whether I was who I said I was. They simply believed me. In any event, I wasn't asking them for anything. Soon, I became a well-known sadhu in the area. I rented a small place near the temple – basic but clean. The food wasn't bad either.

My usual garb was a saffron kurta and lungi, sometimes only a lungi. I had a few cotton and denim shorts with large pockets that I wore underneath. One of the pockets carried my Blackberry – my only contact with the outside world. The friend, with whom I had banked the balance of the pilfered arsenal, would pay the bills and keep the line connected, and look for some big job for me. We largely communicated through encrypted emails.

In my other pocket, I carried one of the Glocks, for I was afraid that the politician or his goons might still be looking for me. A Glock 17 has 9 mm, 124-grain pellets. Seventeen rounds. It was a diminutive handgun, but among small handguns, the Glock 17, a little more than a seven-inch toy and less than a kilogram, was regarded as one of the world's most accurate weapons. Quite like the Bose speakers – not the best, but the very best in the *small-sized* category. The Glock was quite precise. Not like a rifle, but then again, it was never designed for long-range big game hunting. I'd trust it for a distance of fifty feet. No more. And it shot at a velocity of over a whopping 1100 feet per second. And that was enough if the politician sent his goons to threaten me, or persuade me to do anything I didn't want to. If they wanted to use a sniper to drop me dead, they would have done it long ago, but I knew they wouldn't. My utility for them wasn't over yet.

I wasn't expecting it so quickly, but I got the message for a new job from my friend a month and a half into my ascetic life. It sounded unlike anything I had done in the past, but the estimated payment offered was more than anything I'd ever received. I would be turning forty soon, and couldn't spend the rest of my life carrying out petty jobs for others. This deal sounded like it could well be a *Get Out of Jail* card for me.

I took my time planning the whole thing to the minutest detail, and then I retreated to my innocent life at Benares, and waited.

A week later, my Blackberry pinged one evening. The message was directly from the people who were hiring me for the job – *'Meeting fixed for tomorrow, 2 p.m.'* Along with it, an address and directions.

I slipped out from my residence that evening, got a haircut, had my beard trimmed, and bought myself some new clothes. Later, I took a bus to Gorakhpur.

I disappeared from Benares under the cover of night.

3

THE CAPTAIN'S STORY

I was confident I was being watched from the time I took the bus from Benares. No doubt about that in my mind. It could be someone on the bus travelling with me, but I wouldn't know. I wasn't scared, no. But I didn't like being spied on.

This was the first time I'd be doing business with the unscrupulous character I was travelling to meet. I was no puritan, and I knew I was in no position to call anyone dishonest, but there was a marked difference between the person I was going to meet and me. At least I didn't keep up a façade of a squeaky-clean politician serving the people in my constituency. Sure, I was a small-time thief, but at least I wasn't embezzling money from those who were needier than me.

The Gorakhpur bus stop was like any other bus stop in a small, dusty town in Uttar Pradesh. A large space, but every inch was taken up by buses, vendors, people and auto-rickshaws. Its proximity to the railway station had sired enough budget hotels in the area, but I had already been booked into one – Hind Hotel, which was on one of the by-lanes behind the highly congested Railway Station Road. It was clean and had a window air-conditioner unit. I locked my room door, had a long shower and dozed off. I was supposed to wait at the hotel for my next instruction.

It was so soft I thought I had imagined it, the knock on my door around noon.

Two guys, who could have easily been wrestlers in some local arena, stood outside my door. They'd come to take me to their leader. Both were over six feet tall and over 150 kilos each, with shaved heads and thick, walrus moustaches. I didn't have any bags with me and my room bill had been taken care of, so I locked the door, gave the key at the reception and walked out to their waiting cream-coloured Mahindra Bolero. One of them got into the driver's seat; the other took the passenger one. I got into the seat behind the driver. Old habit. The rear-view mirror is angled in a vehicle to facilitate the driver and hence, by sitting behind him, you can check whether you are being tailed without having to noticeably turn around. In that Bolero, as far as I could see, there was no other vehicle following us. Thus, either no one was actually tailing us or they were being really discreet. Actually, if I wasn't being paranoid, it could very well be the former. After all, what did I really know about anything so far? That there was a job being offered to me? That it could earn me a few crores? That it was something about pinching a piece of art? What could I do with such little information?

I put my hand around my back to feel the Glock nestled there, should I need it.

'Where are we going?' I asked the men.

'Deoria,' answered the driver.

'How far is it from here?'

'Roughly fifty kilometres.'

Clearly, neither of my fellow passengers seemed to be sparkling conversationalists. I closed my eyes and dozed off.

I woke up as the car left the tarmac and got on to an unpaved trail, the kind that's spotted with natural speed breakers. The driver, despite his best efforts, could only avoid half the pits and juts; the Bolero went up and down and tilted and straightened. I looked out of the window and saw that we were in the middle of nowhere. We hopped and fell for another twenty minutes before I could see a wall – a boundary wall, chest-height and yellow. It stood like a battlement of what I seemed like a sprawling property. The SUV drove up to the black iron gate built into the wall, guarded by a third wrestler who, from a distance, appeared even bigger than my two travelling buddies. He didn't peep into the car to check who was in it; simply pressed some button and the gate began sliding open to let us in. We drove into massive unpaved forecourt dotted with unattended shrubs. They didn't give the impression of having been carefully chosen at a nursery and purposefully planted. The trees were mainly a combination of banyan, deodar, shisham and some others I couldn't identify, besides a lone tamarind – the usual biota of rural north India. The house itself was equally gargantuan as the forecourt – a large, newly built mansion. We parked and got out of the car. I was ushered into the house without so much as a cursory pat, let alone a security check.

Inside, I stood in a more-than-generous-sized living room. A wall of people – associates and cronies and servants and security – greeted us.

The room itself was sparsely furnished. There were four armchairs, a large table covered with a layer of fine dust, a few insignificant wall hangings and the usual, useless bits-and-bobs that sycophants looking to curry favours usually bring as gifts for the politician they are visiting. The house looked impersonal; it could well have been one of those dime-a-dozen banquet halls or lobbies in nondescript hotels.

One of the many men in the room stepped forward and introduced me to the man of the hour, Shri Udhham Kumar, aka Udhham Bhai, a minister in the state assembly. His portfolio was recited to me, perhaps in a bid to impress, but it sounded useless. I took in the man who was the reason I was here.

Even if I had seen him in the backseat of a Rolls Royce, Udhham Kumar would still look like a goon. I knew he was dirty, and sometimes your looks didn't belie you. He had accumulated a lot of money, all under the guise of public service. Bribes, kickbacks, illicit businesses, hawala, blackmailing and whatnot; the guy reeked of greed and corruption.

But what was worse was that the man had zero personality, and even surrounded by cronies and security, didn't make an impression at all. He radiated no authority himself; only the bodyguards he had bought with his rotten wealth confirmed his position in the hierarchy. The left side of his face was covered in pockmarks and the right side had a scar that ran all the way from the earlobe to the chin. I gathered he must have taken a knife to the face. He was wearing a short-sleeved shirt with a few top buttons open, so that his unruly grey fur was on display. His eyes were mean; a reflection of his soul, perhaps. His eyebrows were bushy enough to shame a squirrel's tail. The guy clearly didn't believe in grooming; one of those people who loved money even more than he loved himself.

'Hello, Captain,' he said, sticking his hand out to shake mine. 'I've heard so much about you.' He motioned for me to take a seat.

We sat across each other, sipping the salted lassi that had been served to just the two of us. The other insignificant people in the room got nothing, but they still stood in attendance, watching us. Udhham Bhai couldn't stop making a show of his power.

'I hope you don't believe everything people say. I'm a small-time guy.'

'You are being modest, Captain. My sources have told me that you have the best hands in the country.'

Most unscrupulous people were connected either through various nefarious activities or other equally vile people. They competed with each other, but usually ended up using the same manpower and resources. This also meant that often, they recommended people to each other for stealth jobs. In this case, as my friend had already told me, I had been recommended to Udhham by someone I had worked for before.

'The job I have for you is rather big,' he said. If nothing, I appreciated that the man wasn't wasting any time before getting to the point.

He gave a near imperceptible nod and his pugs sashayed out of the room, leaving me in the company of Shri Udhham Kumar and the two hoodlums, who had come to pick me up at Gorakhpur.

It was then that I finally learned what painting it was that Udhham wanted me to track down – Vincent van Gogh's *Poppy Flowers*. He told me about how the painting had belonged to a Nawab, and passed on to his son, from whose collection it had reportedly gone missing after he'd defaulted on his debts. At least, that was what the Nawab claimed, but Udhham also added that the man could very well be lying. *Poppy Flowers* could still be with him.

Anyway, Udhham's sources had narrowed down the list of people who could have the painting to four. The first two on the list were businessmen – one an infamous wholesale liquor distributor and the other a retailer with a gambling empire behind the front. Albeit dangerous men, both claimed to be art collectors and investors. The third party on the list were two brothers – politicians of ill repute. The fourth name on the list was, of course, the Nawab himself.

'Vincent van Gogh!' I couldn't believe what I was hearing. How is it that a painting of his ended up in India? And honestly, while I had come prepared and knew that I was being asked to steal *a* painting, the fact that it was a *Van Gogh* painting was blowing my mind.

Udhham went on, and told me that he had a buyer in Japan, who was very interested in buying the painting.

'And how much is he going to pay for it?'

'Close to 200 million US dollars, plus change.'

'What do I get?'

'Ten million dollars.'

I felt my heart quicken. That was a cool fifty crore rupees.

'That's more than you will ever make picking the small pockets that you routinely do, Captain,' Udhham said, rightly reading my thoughts.

'And what if I refuse?'

His smile disappeared. He had given me all the details, and now he couldn't afford to let me walk away.

'I'll start by breaking your teeth.'

'And then?'

'Then what?' he barked.

'You said you'd start by breaking my teeth. What would you break next?'

'Smartass, are we?'

'I just wanted to know the chronology,' I retorted. I needed the money just as desperately as he needed me, but it was good practice to establish early on that I wasn't going to be a yes-man. Even if I agreed to work for him, it wouldn't make him my boss.

Udhham gnashed his uneven, yellow teeth, his temper clearly rising. His goons flexed their muscles and moved an inch forward.

'You actually think these pest-control guys can tame me?' I said, but then realised that perhaps it was time to stop baiting Udhham. 'Okay, you want me to work for you, and I am ready to. But I want to make it clear that I don't take well to threats. If that's fine, then we can move forward. If not, I am happy to walk out and I'm sure you'll find a better and much more subservient person to take on this job.'

I could see that he wasn't pleased. He had probably never before been talked to this way. But then I wasn't going to just roll over and give in to intimidation. Sure, I had everything at stake, but he had a lot at stake too.

Thankfully, he stayed calm; did not order his goons to start breaking my teeth. I had my Glock but I didn't want him or anyone else to know that I was carrying it.

Another lassi was asked for and served, and Udhham then took me through what was required of me. First, I'd need to find out who had the painting; then I'd have to steal it, and finally, I'd have to deliver it to him. Simple. He made it sound like he was asking me to steal crayons from an unsupervised kindergarten kid.

I knew that finding out where that dang painting was would be the most difficult part of this job. If the person who owned it had kept it concealed for so long, I'd need to find a way to make him reveal himself now. I said as much, and Udhham cleared his throat to speak.

'How you do that is by—'

'Udhham ji,' I interrupted him, 'the only decision you need to take is if you want me to work on this job or not.'

'What do you mean?'

'I carry out jobs in a manner I am comfortable with and hence, I'll either do it my way or as I mentioned before, I am happy to walk away.' I wasn't playing a game anymore. This was really the way I operated. *I* made the plans and *I* executed them. 'If you want me to do the job, you will have to trust me and let me do it my way. If I need help, I'll ask.'

'You appreciate the odds are stacked against us …' he said.

'I do, and that's precisely why I want to carry out the job in the manner I think is appropriate.'

Udhham nodded and gave me a tight smile.

'So if we do it your way, how long do you think the job will take?'

'Nine months to a year, maybe a little—'

'Are you kidding? There's no way the buyer is going to wait that long!'

'What else can he do? Pull Van Gogh out of the grave and ask him to paint another *Poppy Flowers* just for him? Believe me, Udhham ji, that's the best estimate, if you just want the painting.'

'What do you mean, *just want the painting*?'

'I mean, if you want the painting without getting blood on your hands.'

He furrowed his eyebrows, contemplated the matter and left it at that.

'What about manpower?' he asked after a while.

We were now on the third glass of lassi and my bladder had started protesting.

'As I said, I will ask for resources as and when I need them.'

'But you will need some money in advance, for expenses?'

'Certainly.'

He must have felt confident about me because he didn't blink when I quoted a generous amount.

'Remember, no hanky-panky with me, Captain.'

'You have my word. And besides, you wouldn't just give me an advance and let me go, would you? I am certain that you'll ask your people to keep a watch on me twenty-four/seven.'

He smiled.

'We're friends,' he finally said.

Yes, the kind of shyster friend you wished upon your enemy. But I nodded.

We sat there for two more hours, discussing the task in detail. We worked out the rules and modalities. I was not to contact Udhham directly, but only through Damodar, one of his confidants, and also one of the men who had driven me here.

Finally, after I had been served two more large glasses of lassi, I left.

4
THE CAPTAIN'S STORY

I got down to work almost immediately after I left Udhham in Deoria.

The salient part of the task was to unearth who amongst the four individuals or their families was the de facto current owner of the multi-million-dollar painting. My worry wasn't that Udhham's information was incorrect; my concern was with how up-to-date it was. With the exception of the erstwhile Nawab Jamshed Khan, who had inherited the painting, the other three candidates would have had to acquire it on the sly. And I'm sure that they wouldn't have done so to feed their appreciation of art; it was simply a matter of money for them. Which meant that the painting could have exchanged hands several times since Udhham's sources had got him the information. In any event, even if any of the five named by Udhham still owned the painting, it wasn't like I could walk up to their residence, ring the bell and ask them to show it to me or hand it over.

That was why I became an art professor. It wasn't easy. But then no one makes fifty crores doing a simple job. My gut told me that whoever owned the painting would often wonder if what they had in their possession had any real value. If yes, then how much? The most obvious answer was contacting an art dealer, but then how do you stop the news from spilling once you've engaged a commercial establishment? The art aficionados across the country and the world over would go nuts over something like this. And whoever owned *Poppy Flowers* definitely did not want the world to know.

But an art professor? Now that would be a reasonably safe bet. However, I needed to establish that I was an expert in the Impressionist era, with a keen interest in Van Gogh, and I was the kind of person fit to socialise with people of their ilk.

I flew to Mumbai first. Although I had had my hair cut before I left Benares, it still wasn't half-decent for a professor. An unconventional hair-stylist in Bandra West understood what I was looking for. He parted my hair on the right, left it longer than average, coloured it, and highlighted it with silver. I bought rimless glasses. I wouldn't leave anything to chance, and in any case, it was Udhham Kumar's money that I was spending. Part of the advance had gone towards renting a large house in South Delhi's posh Hauz Khas area. Udhham's men were sorting out the logistics of that while I was in Mumbai, dressing up for the performance of a lifetime. I had asked them to source a few paintings for the house too. An art professor with no art in his home would be odd. I had outlined what I needed and the paintings were supposed to be good, but done by nameless, faceless artists. My intent was to show that I appreciated talent, not names. A car was being organised too – nothing too ostentatious, but something that befitted my status. There had to be some investment in music too. In my mind, there was a connection. You couldn't appreciate just one form of art; its appreciation came in multiple forms – paintings, sculptures, music, all went hand in hand.

I had the clothes, the hair, the house. But the biggest question was, who was I going to *be*?

I spent some time on this, and finally settled on Albert Rueben. It fit the bill perfectly – a near westernised name that suited someone who had lived and worked in Europe. While most people would think the name was Christian, it was, in fact, Jewish. I had done a lot of research, and settled on something that would also work as a conversation piece. I fashioned myself as a forty-plus professor whose parents had passed away. I had no siblings or close relatives in India, and I had once been married to a French woman, but we parted amicably years ago.

In short, I tied up all the loose ends anyone could possibly think of. And, as it is with every new impersonation, I changed my walk, demeanour, smile, style, facial expressions and reactions. I also built a subliminal recognition of the new name I had given myself.

Masquerading as a professor required cerebral work too. I speed read several books – all on art and many that focussed especially on the Impressionist era. I also read about Paris and France and HEC, the previous place I was supposed to have taught at, just in case someone started a conversation about it with me.

Udhham's associates came in handy, and the professor occupying the position I needed at the University was quietly and efficiently removed. They handled the paperwork and references required for the job with élan too.

Mr Albert Rueben was, thus, made to order, and came fully equipped for the job.

5

Udhham Kumar wasn't happy. The gentleness he had shown to the Captain had been masking his fury at the man's insolence, but he'd forced himself to keep his cool. After all, he didn't know if he could find someone else who was skilful enough to dig out the painting and procure it for him. The Japanese buyer he had talked about was genuine, and if Udhham Kumar failed to find someone to do the job, nothing would stop the buyer from going elsewhere and approaching someone else to acquire the same painting for him. Udhham only knew about the Captain, others might know even more efficient people.

But the Captain's behaviour was hardly subservient for someone being paid more money than he'd ever seen in his life. For that amount, Udhham expected a monkey at the end of a rope that danced when ordered.

Once the Captain had left, Udhham turned to Damodar. 'Get Sylvia on the line,' he barked at the man.

Sylvia was Udhham Kumar's advisor-cum-cloak-and-dagger operative for a variety of reasons. He had first met her more than a decade ago, when she used to be a high-end escort in Lucknow. She had disappeared from the scene soon after their first rendezvous, when a high-profile murder took place in the hotel that used to make bookings for her. A few months ago, he had accidentally run into her during a visit to Lucknow. He was in the city for a meeting and was staying at a hotel in Gomti Nagar. She was checking in at the same hotel, and was standing at the reception, dressed like a corporate executive. He had recognised her instantly. Still as gorgeous, just a little older. She either didn't recognise him or didn't want to, for obvious reasons. He waited until she had left. He asked the receptionist for her room number and made the call from his. After a bit of small talk, she said that she wasn't in the escort business now and so, sex was off the table, but agreed to meet him for dinner.

Over dinner, he found out that she worked for some private investigation firm in Mumbai and was in Lucknow for some work.

'Who're you looking into?'

'Sorry, Mr Kumar, but I cannot share that. What I do is highly confidential and clients pay as much for discretion as they do for the information. I hope you'll understand.'

'So this firm … the one you work for, does it employ you full time or only on a case-to-case basis?'

'I am a contractor, so it's on a case-to-case basis.'

'Is it fair to assume that all the work you carry out might not be above board? I mean, it can't all be legal?'

'Why do you want to know that?' she narrowed her eyes.

'Would you work for me?'

'If you are referring to the work I did in my previous life, I'll have to say, forget it—'

'No. I appreciate that you have moved on. I wouldn't want to force myself upon anyone. This is something totally different.'

'I don't see why not. What is it that you want me to find out for you?'

'What if I say I want you to bring me the country's best conman?'

'Now we're talking.' She leaned back. 'Shouldn't we order some drinks?'

He called the waiter and ordered a gin and tonic for Sylvia and a scotch on the rocks for himself.

'So, what do you want a conman for?' Sylvia's finger was twisting a lock of hair that had come loose from the bun she had her hair up in.

'We can discuss the details later. First, you have to agree to take the job.'

'I might even have a few names for you already. But what do I get in return?'

The deal had been simple. Sylvia offered two names. One of the guys operated in Mumbai, the other was a Delhi villain. Udhham had called up his connections and everyone he spoke to confirmed that the Captain would be perfect for the job. He was deft, he was a perfect impersonator, and he had the panache needed to carry out this job.

That settled it.

Udhham had paid Sylvia handsomely for the recommendation and offered her a one-year contract to see the project through. While he did tell her that this was an art heist, he didn't divulge the details.

Now, when Damodar had Sylvia on the line, Udhham confirmed to her that the deal was going ahead with the Captain. Sylvia would need to be in Delhi for the next one year to keep an eye on the guy.

'Me?'

'The guy is sharp, Sylvia. Have you ever met him yourself?'

'No, never.'

'He's expecting that someone will be keeping an eye on him in Delhi, but I doubt he'll expect someone as beautiful as you.'

'Where will he be staying in Delhi?' Sylvia asked, ignoring the compliment.

'I'm getting a house ready for him in Hauz Khas. I want you to fit it up with discreet surveillance equipment. Put them in his car too. That way, if he makes one wrong move, we will know immediately.'

'Sure.'

'And keep out of his way. Under no circumstance should your cover be blown. I cannot afford for this deal to fail.'

'Done.'

'That's my girl,' Udhham said happily.

'Please send me his picture, Udhham bhai.'

'I'll ask someone to text it to you. And Sylvia …'

'Yes?'

'Please don't call me bhai.'

PRESENT DAY

6
THE CAPTAIN'S STORY

It had been six months from the time I had visited Udhham Kumar's Deoria hideaway and agreed to take up the job. I'd been installed in the Hauz Khas house for four months now, and I was still none the wiser about the painting's whereabouts now than I had been six months ago. I was like a drunken spider circling a little area aimlessly. Doubts started sprouting within me like acne on the face of a thirteen-year-old. Honestly, it felt like I was chasing a mirage.

On other fronts, I had no reason to complain. Udhham was paying all my bills for a whole year; I was living in one of the poshest localities in New Delhi and driving around in an Audi A4. Sure, the car would be taken away if I failed to deliver, but I was sure I'd be allowed to keep the custom-made wardrobe.

But the I hated failing. If *Poppy Flowers* was in Delhi, I needed to find it, obtain it, deliver it to Udhham and take the money we'd agreed upon. I recognised that, so far, I'd only been cruising. I needed to floor the pedal now.

Before today, I had only flirted with mentions of Van Gogh in class, throwing his name in with the other greats. Like a true Impressionist art professor, I had started the course with a precursor to the era, and then steered my pupils into Impressionism and the broader characteristics of the movement – its history, the open compositions that provided a sense of movement, the thin yet discernible brush strokes that defined the style, and the precise portrayal of light. So far, I had stuck to the course programme prescribed by the college.

But now, after spending four months establishing my credentials, I knew that I was on terra firma. I decided not to waste any more time waiting for the ball to come to me. I had to chase it. The students in my class were rich, upper-class people who moved in circles I needed to target. If anyone in the city had the painting, I was certain that someone in the class would know someone who'd know something about it.

And I decided to begin with Sheena Marwah. She was kittenish, she was connected, and she was married to some software millionaire, who was forever jet-setting between New Delhi and Palo Alto. After four months, I still hadn't figured out what had brought her to this class. Was she genuinely interested in art or merely looked at it as an investment? Well, if I couldn't be sure about her interest in art, at least I was confident about her interest in me. She was subtle with the flirting, but I could recognise the signs easily. So far, I'd tried to ignore it, but now, it was time to use it.

As I left the class, I told everyone that I had more reading material on Impressionism in my office, should anyone be interested. Everyone was invited to stop by, but it's Sheena I looked at when I made my offer.

And sure enough, she did. An hour later, there was a knock on my office door.

'Come in.'

'Hello, Mr Rueben.' She walked in. She was in good shape, and her shoulder-length, sleek brown hair swung from side-to-side as she walked.

'How may I help you, Sheena?'

'You had mentioned after class that you had some additional reading material on Impressionism that we could…'

'Oh yes, the material! Sorry, I forgot,' I said, as if I hadn't been waiting this whole while for her to show up. I turned around to rummage in the bookshelf behind me. I could feel her eyes on my back.

'Tell me about you,' she said, her voice soft.

'About me?' I turned back to her and cocked an eyebrow.

She nodded, her eyes bright with interest, like I was a piece of art myself.

'Like what? I mean, I am an art professor who was in France until a year ago. I returned to India and spent some time travelling before I picked up this assignment. That pretty much sums up my résumé.'

'Single?'

'Yes. Divorced. What about you?'

'I'm married.' She raised her hand to show me her ring, a platinum band with an obscenely large diamond.

'I know that. I meant, tell me more about *you*.'

'Well, I married early. My parents picked the groom, I wasn't given a choice in the matter. I'm not complaining – I mean, Raj is a great husband. He works hard, provides me with everything I could want. I've travelled more than most ladies in our social circle…'

'And are the others in your social circle also fascinated by paintings and art?' I decided to take control of the conversation before she steered it towards long, detailed descriptions of her travels.

'Not all, but sure, some are. It's Raj and I who are most interested in that sort of thing, though. To be honest, Raj is more interested in the investment aspect of it.'

'So, is there any specific form or period of art you're both interested in or just anything that's a sound investment?'

'Anything, actually. For me, it should be appealing to the senses, but for Raj, it has to be an investment.'

'How does he determine what is a good investment?'

'He keeps up with art journals and news about the art world, but the problem is that by the time he reads a piece of information, everyone else who is interested has read it too. So the prices are already up, you see?'

'That explains why you're here. You need to learn enough to be a step ahead of everyone and help your husband make an informed choice.'

'And you can help me do that,' she said, stood up and walked over to the window. Seeing her up close like this, in my tiny office, I realised that she was captivating in a strange sort of way.

'How?' I asked.

'My husband is travelling. He returns next week. I could take you around this weekend to show you some paintings that are for sale. We can assess them together.' She turned around and looked at me, as if daring me to decline.

'Of course,' I agreed immediately. This was the opening I'd been looking for, after all. I had been to check out an art gallery on my own a couple of months back, and introduced myself to the gallery owner as an art professor. That didn't break a lot of ice; the owner gathered within minutes that I wasn't there to buy. But with Sheena by my side, we'd get a lot of attention, and it wasn't a big leap to think that whoever owned the Van Gogh might have spoken to someone in the art trade. It was not a sure shot, but it was better than sitting at home.

'So, are you free this weekend?' she asked as she fluttered back to her chair.

'Indeed I am.'

'Great. I could pick you up in the morning?'

I gave her my address. She noted it down, showed me her polished incisors, slipped out of the chair, and cat-walked out of my office, leaving behind a faint trace of the floral fragrance she was wearing.

I took out my Blackberry and started typing.

Sheena was at my doorstep at nine on Saturday morning. We hadn't decided on the time, but I had been expecting her after ten or thereabouts. So when she arrived, I was still in bed. I jumped at the bell and saw her through the window of the living room.

'Good morning!' She was bright and cheerful when I opened the door. 'Not ready yet, Mr Rueben?'

'I apologise,' I said, stepping aside to let her into the living room.

She was dressed to kill, wearing a sleeveless, light linen summer dress in pure white that clung to her body and didn't leave much to my imagination. Shin-high, open-toed tan sandals drew attention to her smooth legs and perfectly pedicured feet. I gestured towards the sofa in the living room and walked behind her.

'Coffee?' I asked.

'Show me the kitchen. I'll make it while you change?'

I didn't want her in my house for too long, but it wasn't like I had a choice. So I showed her the kitchen and the ingredients and then left to take a quick shower. I locked, and double-checked my bedroom before I undressed. I didn't want any complications. Being fed morsels of playfulness and peekaboo was acceptable, but a romp with a married woman would sooner or later lead her husband to my door and that was the last thing I wanted – nuisance that drew attention to me.

I was back in fifteen minutes, clad in jeans, a pale blue shirt and moccasins.

'Your coffee is ready. How do you take it?'

'Black, no sugar. Thanks.'

'Same as me!' She exclaimed like this was a one-in-a-million coincidence.

'I guess so.'

We finished our coffees, and were out in ten minutes.

'Where shall we go?' She sat in the car and put on her expensive tortoise shell glasses. Her linen dress hiked up, exposing more leg.

'I thought you were the guide. Let's go wherever you think there are paintings good enough for you to buy.'

The first gallery, which was a kilometre from my house in Hauz Khas, was a total dump. It allegedly specialised in featuring the works of contemporary, abstract artists; nothing but paint-splashed canvasses, the meaning of which only the artist could interpret. The gallery owner did not seem to know anything either. All he did was confirm my suspicion that most gallery owners were as ignorant as the people who bought from them. Intermittently, he stole lewd glances at Sheena, and tried his best to take her address to build a database of rich clientele that he could pester later.

'I don't think you deal in the kind of paintings we are looking for,' I said curtly, and walked out.

The second and the third art galleries didn't have anything remarkable either. They carried equally inane paintings from disillusioned artists. I asked the owners if they or anyone they knew had paintings from the previous periods – Renaissance, Romanticism, Impressionism, Cubism – but drew a blank. Okay, expecting paintings of those eras at these galleries was a bit ambitious. This was turning into a futile expedition.

We moved on.

'Lunch?' Sheena asked.

'Why not?' I glanced at my watch. It was past one, and I was beginning to get hungry.

We were near the Defence Colony market in South Delhi, so decided to find a place there. We parked, walked into a Chinese restaurant and helped ourselves to the ongoing all-you-can-eat buffet.

'Now you understand our problem?' Sheena said after we'd taken our seats.

'What problem?' I looked up from my plate.

'We have the money, but there isn't much that's worth buying.'

'I'm sure there is. We'll find something.'

Just as I turned back to my plate, she broke into a fit of giggles.

'What now?' I realised I was smiling too.

'I ... can't believe ... you were actually asking them ... about art from that period ...' she said between chuckles.

'Well, apart from being an old git, I like art from that period like some people prefer films from the old black-and-white era, so I thought—'

'You're not that old!' Sheena protested.

As we ate, the conversation segued into whatever caught Sheena's fancy.

After lunch, we made our way to the fourth gallery, which was also in Defence Colony. This one had a few good paintings and sculptures. The owner too seemed a bit more clued in.

Sheena took a shine to the nudes. And to be honest, some of them, by a not-so-prominent artist, were really brilliant – vivid and intense.

'What do you think of this one?' she pointed towards one that had a woman sitting on a stool, looking at herself in the mirror. She was completely naked and her back was painted so exquisitely that it looked like a photograph; her face was visible in the mirror.

'Overbearing is how I'd describe it,' I said.

'Why? She's beautiful!'

'I know. The artist should have stopped at her. He didn't need to paint the rest of the canvas, which is garish and the contrast is harsh.'

Sheena pursed her lips and nodded slowly, moving on to the next painting.

'Why is this one so expensive?' She turned and asked the gallery owner, who was walking behind us, probably admiring Sheena's derrière. The canvas showed an anorexic female in the nude, dancing in some imaginary forest, her private parts covered with branches of colourful bougainvillea. Hardly an imaginative concept, but well painted, nevertheless.

The Dancing Corpse's price tag boasted a figure close to nine lakhs, minus some change that could buy you a hair clip if you weren't particular about quality.

'This is Remi Malhotra's last work. He passed away last month,' he explained, his tone melancholic, like a close relative had died. All theatrics to hike up the price, clearly. He started telling us a sappy story about how Remi fell in love, got rejected, stopped painting and drank himself to death. The whole thing reminded me of the script of *Leaving Las Vegas,* where Nicholas Cage drank himself to his end, but I kept shut.

It wasn't the best piece in the gallery. But that was something time would correct, I knew. If Remi had lived longer and painted more canvases, *The Dancing Corpse* might possibly have been relegated to someone's basement. But now, after his death, I could sense that the appreciation on this would be disproportionately higher, and a great deal faster.

'Do you know Mr Rueben is an art professor, Mr…?' Sheena's voice broke into my thoughts.

'Deepak Mehta. Where do you teach, Mr Rueben?' the owner asked.

Before I could reply, I heard Sheena introducing me as an authority on Impressionist art. She went on to highly embellish my profile … that I had been head of department at a French university that I had never heard of, that I was a member of some UN Arts Council that may or may not have existed … Sheena could talk. I turned back to the painting as she went on.

'You seem very taken by this one, Mr Rueben,' I heard Mehta say to me. 'Isn't it great?'

'It is good, indeed, but it's also overpriced.'

'What are you saying, Professor Sahib? Remi is no more…'

'Is that all there is? I mean, is there any other reason besides that?'

'A piece like this will never be in the market again,' Mr Mehta declared dramatically.

'I know that, but still.'

'Ramesh,' Mehta called his assistant, 'get us some drinks … what will you have?' he asked us. He was a good salesman. He had gauged our interest. He had figured out Sheena had the money. He was moving in to make a hard sell, to close the deal.

'Coffee for us. Two blacks, no sugar please.' Sheena ordered for both of us.

Coffees were served and savoured, negotiations took place, and the price of the painting was locked down at seven lakhs. Sheena booked it but said she needed to speak to her husband before buying such an expensive piece. Then she took a photo of it and sent it to him.

I picked up the topic of period paintings. Mehta had woolly knowledge, but claimed that his father – who had run this gallery for over forty years and had only just retired – would know more. But the older man only came to the gallery on weekday mornings.

'Could I have his number? I'd like to speak with him,' I said.

'Of course, he'd love to talk to you.'

We left after six. Mr Mehta came out of the gallery to see us off.

'Home?' Sheena asked once he'd left.

'I'll take a cab,' I responded.

'You don't like my company?' She pouted.

'Of course I like your company.'

'How much?'

She was relentless, wasn't she?

'Enough to spend the day with you,' I said. 'Do you think your husband will like *The Dancing Corpse*?'

'Changing the topic, are we?'

You do it all the time, sweetheart. 'Not at all. Didn't I say I enjoyed your company all day today?'

'So why not have dinner with me?'

This was getting ridiculous. I knew that I was about to become another feather in her cap. I could envisage her telling her friends or other students in my class: *'You know, the other night, Mr Rueben and I went out for dinner … No, no, my husband wasn't there, just him and me.'*

'Okay,' I heard myself say.

'There were some interesting paintings in your house, I'd like to come around some day and have a closer look.'

I simply smiled as she turned the key in the ignition.

7

Sub-inspector Hari Mohan Gupta was an upright police officer, and that was his only drawback. He was clever enough to realise the irony – being good had been very bad for him.

He was an unusual case of an apple falling so far from its tree that it was no longer even acknowledged by anyone as ever having been a part of it. Hari Mohan's father, Ram Mohan, a small time crook attached to a bigger crook of a politician, had been as corrupt a person as they come.

Consequently, Hari Mohan left home when he was seventeen, taking his mother along. Terrified that they might be hunted down and brought back by Hari Mohan's fathrer, the mother and son renounced Meerut and moved to Delhi. Jamunabai took up menial jobs while her son worked part time and carried on with his studies.

To Hari, having had no real exposure to life so far, a police officer seemed like the epitome of righteousness and morality. And so, he became one. He joined the force as a constable and despite his hard labour, got no promotion for the first twenty-two years of service. Instead, he earned a reputation for being incorruptible. He frequently got verbal compliments from the senior officers, but was transferred soon after. If they ever awarded a policeman for being reassigned to the maximum number of police stations, Hari Mohan would have beaten everyone hands down. He abhorred corruption in any shape and form; it gave him sleepless nights. He didn't like the bureaucracy and bureaucracy kindly returned the favour.

Five-foot-nine, broad-shouldered, balding with a few stray grey strands, and now in his late fifties, he was headed towards retirement after having made it to the rank of sub-inspector. His mother had passed away, daydreaming that her son would one day bring in a daughter-in-law, but that wasn't meant to be. Sub-inspector Hari Mohan Gupta was a confirmed bachelor.

And he was very peeved at the moment. He was stationed in the Burari Chowk Police Station on the Outer Ring Road, and had led an enquiry into a police chase where two police field officers had followed a criminal but had failed to nab him. The said that the criminal in question had been transporting stolen police weaponry, and after months of enquiry, the case had gone cold.

Hari knew that he wouldn't find peace until he tracked down the stolen police weapons. When he came to know that a life-long criminal – one Vagh Pratap Singh aka the 'Captain' – was allegedly involved, but had since then relinquished the path of crime and surrendered himself to the service of God, he couldn't buy it. The whole thing stank. From what they knew of him, this sudden transformation to spirituality did not fit the personality of the Captain. Something had to be brewing, though there wasn't anything yet on the surface. But Hari Mohan believed in the Captain's change of heart as much as he believed in Santa Claus.

And while Hari Mohan might not have liked the police machinery and its politics, he sure loved his job. He never did anything half-heartedly. With one year to go before his retirement, Sub-inspector Hari Mohan Gupta swore that if he put only one more criminal behind bars, it would be Vagh Pratap Singh.

'He's romancing a flippin' bird?' Udhham Kumar lost his temper and the control on his volume all at once; his stomach churned as he heard about the Captain's girlfriend, and how the two had spent the day visiting art galleries, lunching and dining. 'I'm paying through my bloody nose, waiting for him to deliver, and he's rolling in the hay with someone's wife?'

'Not really,' Sylvia said in a soothing voice, trying to calm him down.

'What then? You said this girl came to the Hauz Khas house, they had coffee and he left with her for the day, didn't you? That they only returned late night?'

'Calm down, Udhham bhai…'

'And you, I told you not to call me bhai!' he shouted, and then in a softer voice, said, 'I'm sorry. It isn't your fault that the bastard is wasting time and money.'

'She's his student. Sheena Marwah,' Sylvia said.

'Bah! Doesn't he know he'll get unnecessary attention by romancing a student?'

'Okay, you have to listen to the entire thing first, Mr Kumar.'

'That's more like it.'

'What?'

'Mr Kumar.'

'Thank you.'

'No. Thank you, for not calling me bhai. You know we've been—'

'I know. Moving on … Sheena Marwah is a rich socialite, married to Raj Marwah. They reside in New Friends Colony in Delhi, and are loaded, with more money than they can possibly spend. They invest in art, mostly paintings.'

She had his attention now. Udhham was no longer shouting, and Sylvia pressed on.

'My assumption is – remember they did not drive in Captain's car or I would have heard more – that she wants him to assess some paintings. Maybe wants to buy some.'

'How does that help us? That woman isn't looking for the same Vincent van Gogh painting, I suppose?'

'If she is, then they are definitely looking in the wrong places. Van Gogh's missing masterpiece wouldn't be displayed with a "For Sale" sign in an art gallery's window. No, I think the Captain has a bigger plan, though I can't tell you what it is.'

'Hmm…'

'I'm sorry, but they did not have much of a conversation at home or I would have caught it on the transmitters.'

'I'll ask him to take his own car the next time.'

'I wouldn't advise that, Mr Kumar. I know you said he knows that he might be under surveillance, but he doesn't know to what extent. If he suspects that his car is bugged, he'd be wary of saying anything when he's in it. Moreover, he might suspect that his home is bugged too, and we might lose all the hush-hush info we are getting right now.'

'You are smart, Sylvia.'

'Thank you, Mr Kumar.'

'Any chance we could get together just one more time?'

'No, bhai.'

'Well, there was no harm in trying, was there? So, this Sheena, how old is she?'

'Thirty, maybe.'

'Is she good looking?'

'She is gorgeous.'

'What if the Captain falls in love with her and forgets about the job?'

'She's married, Mr Kumar.'

'Oh, don't tell me that makes a difference.'

'Sure, but why would Sheena give up on a multimillionaire for a much poorer art professor?'

'Hmm…'

'And from whatever I've heard about the Captain, he isn't going to trade fifty crore rupees for a woman, however dazzling.'

'You have a valid point, as always. Keep on top of the situation. Call me if you hear anything. If he wavers even a centimetre from the plan, tell me and I'll send the boys.'

'Don't you worry, Mr Kumar.' Sylvia's voice was smooth.

Click.

For all the rage he had felt at the beginning of the call, Udhham Kumar was now pleased. The Captain's methods might have been different, but the guy was clearly trying to get close to the painting by all means. After all, he did think there was a neat fifty crores in it for him.

Fifty crores? Udhham burst out laughing. He had no intention of giving that smartass Captain a single paisa after the painting was delivered. He'd ask his boys to finish the guy and bury him where even the wild animals couldn't find his carcass. He'd rather use that money to take Sylvia in as his mistress. The Captain would be of no use after the job, whereas Sylvia could serve him for another ten-fifteen years. And if she didn't want to be a kept woman, there were always other jobs he could create for her. Considering she was an expert in judo, she could be his bodyguard, and stay close to him. And he'd make her wear the shortest, tightest hot pants…

8

THE CAPTAIN'S STORY

I had taken a week off from work.

Not that I needed one, but every other professor at the college was taking time off and I didn't want to do anything to draw attention to myself. Already, the fact that Sheena was dining with me when her husband wasn't in town had got people talking, and I needed to make sure I didn't give them more fodder. Although after I had dinner with her, I realised that Sheena had no interest in developing any kind of illicit relationship with me, or any other man for that matter. My initial assessment of her hadn't been too far off the mark – all she wanted was attention, and for everyone else to believe that she was a wild card; that she had more close male friends than her friends. Maybe there was a scorecard among the rich socialites? She loved to tease, to attract attention, to score points over her friends. I didn't know why, and I didn't care.

I managed to speak to the older Mr Mehta, the gallery owner Deepak Mehta's father. I told Prakash Mehta that a close friend of mine had recently bought an expensive piece,

The Dancing Corpse, from his son's gallery, and as I was an art professor, I received a lot of queries from other buyers, who were also looking to invest in art. He didn't invite me to meet him and that was okay. Why drive when Alexander Graham Bell had spent his life inventing a brilliant device for us? Unfortunately, that device helped me find out that Mr Mehta suffered from verbal diarrhoea. Once he started talking, he wouldn't stop, despite my million attempts at trying to steer the course of the conversation towards what I needed to know. It was evident that no one had visited him or contacted him in the recent times about any period art. Other than that, he was a fountain of useless information. I kept alternating the phone between my ears to avoid getting a headache from his raspy voice. I could tell by his voice and the persistent coughing and wheezing that he had clearly been a twenty-a-day kind of smoker for decades.

He told me about a friend, another art gallery owner, who was more informed about the art world than he was. I shuddered at the very thought of having to go through an identical conversation with another art loony, but took down his friend's number, thanked the man and promised him that I'd come down one of these days to see him personally.

As I'd expected, and feared, Mehta Senior's friend sucked my brain like an industrial vacuum cleaner until I could feel the lightness in my skull. Forty minutes later, all I got from him was some more inane information and a number for another art gallery owner.

Who said that the life of crime was an easy one?

Mr Mehta's friend's friend had other friends.

Seven such friends later – and it took me three days to get through them – I was no further from where I had been at the start. None of those people had received any enquiries about a painting from the Impressionist era in the past decade.

The last one of Mr Mehta's friends had given me a reference of an art connoisseur and multimillionaire collector, Mr Jhunjhunwala. He was travelling and would only return to India over the weekend. But given how things were going, at best, Jhunjhunwala would give me a reference of yet another art lover or seller, I thought.

On Wednesday, I decided to drive around to the homes of the four names on the list of *Poppy Flower's* potential owners.

The first, Bipin Patel, was the reverse of *Panchatantra*'s fabled coloured jackal. He was a hyena, but he wanted people around him to believe that he was a gentle, harmless lamb, and for the most part, he was successful. He had built a biosphere around him that only showcased his respectable persona as an owner of kosher businesses – retail and distribution of mobile phones and computing, and a nationwide transportation firm that ran a fleet of lorries. The legitimate businesses made money, but they weren't even a distant second to his main occupation. Bipin Patel was one of the most dangerous men in the country.

Back in Mumbai, he had been referred to as the 'Matka King'. It wasn't legal, but like most illegal activities, one had to be either caught red handed or the police needed to have evidence against you. Mumbai Police might have known the colour of Bipin Patel's briefs but they couldn't pull them down. And they never found anyone with the balls to testify against him.

Then Bipin Patel moved to Delhi, set up legitimate businesses, became an art aficionado, joined the social clubs, and came to be accepted as an upright man.

He lived in a two-and a-half acre farmhouse in Chhatarpur. The property had a six-foot high boundary wall all around to keep away enemies and any prying. He had also had round-the-clock security.

There was no way I could sneak into his farmhouse to search for the painting, and return without his men popping a bullet in my head.

The second possible owner of the painting, JK Prasad, was a liquor distributor for Delhi and Uttar Pradesh. I knew enough to know that you couldn't run that business if you didn't have manpower and clout. He had been a known art collector for decades, and he, too, stayed in a farmhouse in Sainik Farms, with enough security to prevent anyone like me from breaking in.

The third name on my list was actually two names; a pair of dubious brothers. Rajdeep and Baldev Singh had criminal affiliations too. They might not have been as dangerous on the surface as the first two, but were just as vile. They weren't politicians themselves, but were henchmen for a dangerous and powerful politician. Not like that made the brothers any less impressive. They were involved in all sorts of activities any decent man would be embarrassed to be associated with. And again, penetrating their fortress of a house in Vasant Vihar was unimaginable for me.

Finally, there was the junior Nawab. He still lived in an old-style kothi on Prithviraj Road. The real estate there was stupendously expensive, but the house itself looked like it could do with some serious repair. The Nawab and his ancestors might have been rich once, but were clearly strapped for cash now. One look at the outside and I felt like writing them a cheque for a new lick of paint. I was certain that there was no way the owner of that building was sitting on a painting worth 200 million US dollars. On instinct, I wrote him off.

Even if the other men on my list had possession of the painting, it did not mean that it would be in the residence that they currently lived in. And that wasn't my only challenge. It could well be that the painting had possibly changed hands and was with someone else altogether by now. It wasn't like Udhham Kumar's information was being updated daily.

What had I signed up for?

My week-long vacation was over and I was back in class.

Mr Jhunjhunwala, the art collector, never returned my call. I tried once again, but then let it go; there seemed little point in pursuing him. If he wasn't interested in returning my calls, why would he be enthusiastic in talking to me about what paintings he owned or knew about?

After class, Sheena dropped into my office to tell me that her husband had loved the painting – *The Dancing Corpse* – and that he wanted to meet me to thank me personally.

'That's not required. You were the one who identified the right piece of art. I only went along with your choice.'

'He still wants to meet you.'

'Why?'

'Why not? It will be good. He adores the painting we bought. I think he wants to pick your brains for other purchases.'

'Well…'

'You sound disinterested. Is it something I said?'

'No, it's just that I know your husband travels a lot and I feel I'm infringing on the little time you get with him.'

'But we'll enjoy your company.'

'*We?* He hasn't even met me.'

'He's been married to me long enough to enjoy what I enjoy.'

'Oh, I see.'

'So, we'll see you this Friday? Why don't you come over to our place and then we can go out for dinner?'

I conceded.

9

'Mumbai?' Udhham Kumar asked, louder than he had intended. He had instructed Sylvia to stay put in Delhi for the length of the assignment, discreetly following the Captain and listening to his conversations. Sure, he had been explicit about her not contacting him. She was to remain invisible at all times and ergo, maybe it didn't matter if she needed a short vacation out of town – the surveillance would still remain in place to capture the Captain's move, so why was he worrying? Plus, she was asking for permission; she hadn't just flown off. He lowered his voice and softened his tone. 'Why do you need to go to Mumbai?'

'I have a feeling something big is about to happen…'

He waited for her to continue.

'And I'd like to visit my church in Mumbai before that.'

'Oh, but there are many churches in Delhi, and anyway, as they say, God is everywhere,' he said, trying to brush her off.

'There are churches, and there is *my* church,' she was firm.

'When do you plan to go?'

'I'm booked on tomorrow morning's flight.'

'That's really short notice, Sylvia.'

'I know, and I'm sorry, but I need to do this.'

'And when will you be back?'

'In two days.'

'Do I need to arrange for someone to watch over the Captain for those two days?'

'Honestly, no, you don't. I'll still keep tracking his conversations, and notify you if there's anything unusual. So far, I don't think there's going to be any change in the next two days,' she assured him.

'I still can't trust this guy, you know.'

'Then why don't you just fire him and get someone else, Mr Kumar?' Sylvia suggested.

'I can't. Not now.'

'Why not now? What's changed?'

'Too much is already invested in him, Sylvia. We are already seven months into a twelve-month commitment. We get a new guy in on the job, we waste time in explanations, negotiations, and then he will have his own theory and tactics for the heist.'

'But if you can't trust the Captain, the sooner we hire someone else and get started, the better,' she argued.

'What I'm worried about is that the Captain doesn't look like the kind of guy who'd stop because I tell him to. He might carry on with his own little private mission and that could be a problem for us. The last thing we want is too many people probing around for *Poppy Flowers*, and before we know it, someone else takes it from under our bloody noses.'

'So, what you're saying is that we are stuck with him?'

'No, but we cannot take a decision of firing him in haste. I don't want him to remain a loose end... someone who knows about it and comes back to bite us in our ass even after the painting is sold. Whoever owns it will not stop the search. If we antagonise the Captain, he might sell me out to the owner. He knows who I am now.'

'Could *you* not find out where the painting is?'

'If I could, I wouldn't have wasted a rupee on that smartass Captain. He was hired to find and filch it, and seven months into the job, he hasn't even completed the first part.'

'Mr Kumar, what are my orders, then? Can I go to Mumbai for a couple of days?' Sylvia said, getting back to the question on hand.

'Yes, you can. But see if you can try and return a bit earlier. Don't worry about the expenses.'

'Roger that, Mr Kumar. Sylvia, the shadow, will stalk him like a ghost.'

After hanging up, Udhham reflected on what he had told Sylvia. He was shrewd enough to recognise that the Captain wouldn't simply drive over to Udhham's Deoria residence, hand over the painting and collect his fee. He'd probably want his share before he handed the painting over, and Udhham would want possession of the painting before he dispensed the cash. There was already a conflict of interest, even before they knew where the painting was.

The only way Udhham could think of tilting the scales in his favour was to send Damodar – his trusted confidant – to Delhi the moment the whereabouts of *Poppy Flowers* were known. Damodar, along with Sylvia, could follow the Captain until he procured the painting, and then waste the guy and bring Udhham the painting. He was confident that Damodar and Sylvia together could easily overpower the Captain.

Sub-inspector Hari Mohan Gupta felt like he was on a pilgrimage. Tracing the Captain's movements had first taken him to Benares's Kaal Bhairav temple, where he'd discovered that, before arriving in the city, the Captain had first visited Pushkar for a brief sojourn. So now, the sub-inspector was in Pushkar, also known as 'Tirtha Raj', the king of all pilgrimage sites, best known for its Brahma temple.

Hari Mohan's career might have stagnated, but that was no reflection of his mental aptitude. Now, his gray cells were working overtime. Why had the Captain come here and then moved to Benares? If the Captain had no ulterior agenda and truly sought peace, Benares was as good as any other place. Why come to Pushkar first?

He knew of the Captain's history – his association with Ajmer, his father's murder; the police files had it all. It was a gloomy start to life, but as far as Hari Mohan was concerned, that did not grant anyone a right to become a criminal.

For a second, Hari Mohan toyed with the idea that the Captain had really reformed. It was certainly a possibility, but it was still one that was hard to swallow, at least until Hari Mohan met the man and looked him in the eye.

And anyway, there was one lone fact that worked against the Captain – if he really had renounced the world of crime, where was he now? Because the Captain, at least in his sadhu avatar, was no longer in Benares.

No, Hari Mohan had no reason to give up the chase. Not yet.

10

THE CAPTAIN'S STORY

Sheena's New Friends' Colony home was an enormous white plastered house; its curved features, circular windows and black brick renderings giving it an art deco feel. There was a large balcony above the ground floor that seemed to be accessible from the bedrooms on the first. The gate was black iron, and had a watchman. Inside, there was an enviable garden blooming with lush plants and a gravel walkway that took me to the main door.

Sheena answered the door before I got to it. The watchman had probably communicated my arrival. She looked even more stunning than usual, dressed to the nines in a salmon-pink, figure-hugging dress, with matching heels, nails and a single string of pink pearls around her slim, graceful neck.

'Welcome, Mr Rueben,' she said, coming forward to receive the social peck on her cheek.

I walked behind her into their large living room. The house screamed class – tasteful art and style, nothing garish. The whole effect was subtle and dignified.

'Good evening, Mr Rueben.' I heard a male voice behind me. A tall, handsome man, five-eleven maybe, stretched out his hand for a shake. 'Raj Marwah,' he said in a smooth, polished voice, his grip firm. He was not much older than Sheena, but his long, coiffed back hair had more grey than usual for his age. Clad in blue jeans, a white shirt and moccasins, he was in semi-casual wear, but his manner and confidence were of someone born into money.

'Hello, Mr Marwah,' I said.

'Raj.'

'Albert.'

'But you are Sheena's professor,' he mocked.

'*Her* professor, not yours … and in *class*, not at dinner…' I looked at Sheena. She smiled back, nodding.

'Apologies for not warning you in advance, but we've called some other friends, another couple—'

'Oh, please don't embarrass me, Raj, it's your house and it will be good to meet some new people anyway.'

'Are you already bored of meeting just me?' Sheena said, batting her eyes. A typical question from her, but I still felt uncomfortable, considering her husband was right there.

'Should I fix you a drink, Albert?' Raj saved me from responding. He didn't seem to mind Sheena's light flirting.

'Yes, please. Whisky. Thanks, Raj.'

'So who are these friends coming for dinner tonight?' I asked Sheena, as Raj walked away to get the drinks and we sat down in the living room.

'Raj's college buddy Arun Jhunjhunwala, and his wife Aditi.'

'Jhunjhunwala?'

'You know them?'

'No.'

Was he the same guy I had been trying to get in touch with the week before? The art collector who was referred to me by one of Prakash Mehta's contacts? I had left my name and number for Jhunjhunwala to call me back when he returned to India, but he hadn't. Either he hadn't received my message or didn't think I was important enough to call back. In any case, Albert Rueben wasn't a common name. If he was the same man, and he had received my message, he would know who I was.

'They are one of the biggest leather exporters in the country,' Raj said as he returned to where we were seated, pushing a small drinks trolley. He made a drink for his wife, a gin and tonic, before pouring whiskies for both of us: Oban. 'Ice, soda or water?' he asked.

'Just ice, please. Thanks.'

'Arun and I were batchmates in college. Aditi and he have a considerable interest in art, like Sheena and I.'

'It's his dad's collection, though,' Sheena spelt out.

'Yeah, his dad has been an art collector and investor for over five decades, so Arun, obviously benefitted from that, but he is a genuine patron himself too.'

Ah, so it might be the same Jhunjhunwala.

Something chimed in the background.

'It must be them.' Sheena walked to an intercom on the side of the main door and spoke to – I presumed – the watchman. 'It's them,' she announced a moment later, replacing the receiver.

Aditi and Arun Jhunjhunwala could have walked into a made-for-each-other couple contest and won it hands down. They weren't half as glamorous as the Marwahs, but they complimented each other. Both were in white and blue. There was nothing in their faces that stood out, but there was a sheen that spoke of opulence and contentment. I guessed that this was the social circle that Sheena mentioned so often in class – prosperous, well established, high-heeled.

Our introductions didn't suggest that Arun had heard my name before.

But in the conversation over drinks, it became evident that the Mr Jhunjhunwala I had called was Arun's father, Amar Jhunjhunwala. He was the one who had recently returned from a trip abroad.

'Oh, I've been trying to contact him, but haven't managed to reach him yet,' I said.

'He's not been well, Albert. I apologise on his behalf. We don't tell people, but he had gone abroad for treatment, not business.'

'I'm sorry. Is he better now?' I asked, all concern and understanding.

'We aren't sure. I mean, he had a liver transplant last year, but the surgery did not heal as smoothly as we had hoped. Hence, the regular travel.'

The conversation regarding his illness continued until Sheena interjected and turned to me. 'Why were you calling Amar Uncle?'

'All for the love of Impressionist art,' I said, underplaying the chase that had led to him.

'I know someone who owns a piece from that period, actually,' Arun said, and my antennas went up.

'You must be joking,' I said to him, my excitement genuine.

'Nope. Jignesh's father acquired one a few years ago from the grey market,' he said, casually, like it was no big deal.

Now I was really interested. An Impressionist work of art from the illegal channel could only mean one of two things. Either it was a fake or it was the *Poppy Flowers*. Anything else would be too much of a coincidence. After all, how many Impressionist paintings were floating around in India?

'Jignesh Patel?' asked Raj.

'Ugh, he's such a social climber, I can't bear him! Or his wife, for that matter. They give me the creeps. Have you seen the clothes she wears, Aditi?' Sheena took off on another tangent.

'You bet, and she can't help showing off her jewellery at every given chance…'

Patel… I shut out the chatter around me and tried to concentrate on the name – *Patel.* Was this Patel related to Bipin Patel, the presumed owner of the stolen Van Gogh?

'Do you know who the painting is by?' Raj's question broke into my thoughts.

'He told me it's a genuine Vincent van Gogh … it's got flowers on it, some flowers—'

'*Poppy Flowers*,' Sheena looked at me, her eyes bright.

'How do you know that?' Raj asked his wife.

'Raj, I am an art student. Albert told us about this painting in the class. Tell them the whole story, Albert. It's quite interesting, guys …' she pressed me.

I mechanically repeated the tale of the museum theft in Egypt, and the stolen *Poppy Flowers*, and how it was still listed as missing. All the while, my mind was churning. I'd found it!

'It's no longer missing, we just found it,' Sheena exclaimed loudly echoing my thoughts.

'But Jignesh's father might not have the original painting. It could easily be a fake, couldn't it?' Raj looked at me.

'Possibly,' I acquiesced. It could only work in my favour. 'Has his father had it examined by an expert?' I asked Arun.

'Nope. His father wouldn't let Jignesh near it, let alone anyone else,' he scoffed.

'Who is his father…? I mean, what's his name? What does he do?' I asked, keeping my voice light.

'Bipin Patel. He has lots of businesses…'

I knew who Bipin Patel was. I knew where he lived. I knew what his *businesses* were. I knew how dangerous he was. And I didn't give a rat's ass about anything else. I now had a confirmation that Bipin Desai was the guy who had directly or indirectly acquired the masterpiece from the Nawab. That was the piece of information I had been in the quest of for the past seven months. I knew getting into a circle of art enthusiasts was the sole amicable tactic to locate the whereabouts of *Poppy Flowers*, and I had been spot on. Bull's bloody eye. It took a while, but then, what didn't? I inherently believed that if you knew where to look, and how, you'd find anyone, including God, although God might be a bit more challenging to find, since too many purported experts were looking to prove his existence in disparate, yet equally irrational, ways. That, and the fact that God didn't carry a mobile phone!

I wondered if my demeanour in any way demonstrated that I was close to nirvana. Then I heard my name.

'Albert, could *you* confirm if Mr Patel's *Poppy Flowers* is genuine or counterfeit?' Sheena asked. I could kiss the girl for bringing up what I hadn't wanted to myself.

'You mean, just with a naked eye inspection?' I asked.

'Yes?'

'I guess, to an extent. I could tell you with at least 99 per cent confidence.'

'Albert is very good …' started Sheena, my self-appointed PR manager, taking a sip of her gin and tonic.

'But if Mr Patel hasn't even shown it to his son, why would he agree to show it to me or any other expert?' I asked.

'I think if my father spoke to Mr Patel, he'd agree. He really respects my dad's opinion,' Amar mused.

'Tell Amar Uncle to call Mr Patel, please? I'd like to see it too!' Sheena had taken the lead here. She was as good as a partner. For her, this was a coup too. If she got to see the painting, she'd come to class with a brass band. Someone in *her* social circle – however distant – owned a *Vincent van Gogh*. OMG!

'Let me see what I can do,' Amar assured her.

'Tell your father that Mr Albert Rueben was a professor in France, and he knows more about Impressionist art than anyone in Delhi, possibly India. It would be in his interest to get it examined to see if he owns the real thing or not, wouldn't it?'

'I will,' reassured Arun.

The evening progressed, admiring the art in the Marwahs' living room. Amongst us all, Arun Jhunjhunwala seemed to be the most well versed in art. Whenever we discussed anything, I read his expressions before opening my gob. I had come this far, and I couldn't afford to let any wrinkle appear in my twenty-four carat reputation as an art professor now.

We didn't go out for dinner. Instead, Sheena called a Thai restaurant and ordered something. Their driver brought it home. We discussed art a little more. I was Mr Ad Lib on vitamins, not steroids; confident, not overbearing. Sometimes, with less, you can get away with more, but it had to be prompt, and correct.

We all exchanged cards. Sheena, once again, reminded Arun Jhunjhunwala about asking his father to call Bipin Patel and arranging a meeting. I was beginning to be really grateful to the girl.

I drove back with my windows down. Enrique Iglesias was telling someone on the radio that he could be their hero and he could kiss away their pain … I smiled. Maybe I could do that too.

I got home, picked up my phone and sent a message – *'Hit Gold. Tell UK?'*

'*Not yet.*' My phone pinged a second later.

I fixed a stiff drink for myself. Finding the painting had taken seven months; that called for a small celebration, didn't it?

11

THE CAPTAIN'S STORY

'Why do you still have it in the tube? Such a thing of beauty ought to be displayed, to be admired!' was the first thing I said when I finally got to see *Poppy Flowers.*

Sheena and I had come to see the painting at Bipin Patel's office in the Kanchenjunga building on Barakhamba Road. No wonder Jignesh, his own son, had never seen the same, since it was kept in a locker in the office. Pity, how some people have all the treasures of the world but no inclination to relish them. How would a hundred-year-old piece of art by a master provide any joy if it was rolled and kept in a tube under lock and key?

Arun Jhunjhunwala had been remarkably expeditious in speaking to his father, who, in turn, spoke to Bipin Patel and agreed to let an expert – me, the art professor, that is – have a look at it and confirm its period and provenance, and since he was convinced what he owned was original, considering its source, he was initially reluctant and put forth his conditions. He asked for some kind of IDs, and copies of our driving licences were sent across to his office. Additionally, as Sheena's family had been known for long enough to the Jhunjhunwala's, in my case he wanted a letter from my college attesting that they employed me. Piece of cake for me to arrange, to be honest.

'I wouldn't have agreed to this, but I cannot say no to Mr Jhunjhunwala. Anyway, I hope you understand this is a one-off, and this information should not leave the room or there will be severe repercussions?' Patel served a stern warning, and his tone, albeit polite, did not leave any doubt that he would carry out his threat if we did anything reckless.

We nodded. We knew – at least I knew – he was a cloaked criminal; Sheena might not have been aware of that, but I wasn't there to highlight to her extra-curricular activities on Bipin Patel's résumé. Each to his own.

He must have been over sixty, but had long black hair – the black reflecting the blue of the dye under the harsh office lights. He had a bushy moustache, also coloured, and his teeth, too, were coloured red from years of paan chewing. He wore an expensive designer suit on his overweight body, which seemed to be stretched beyond its limits. He was exactly as I had imagined – a man looking to be someone he wasn't. He was mesmerised by Sheena, and hardly moved his eyes from her, even as he spoke to me.

'It's more an investment than a showpiece, Professor Rueben,' he replied.

'But even so, no harm in enjoying it as long as you own it.'

'I'm not selling it anytime soon.'

'Of course not.' It was actually better for me that the painting was in a tube. Stealing and carrying a framed painting was a lot trickier.

'So, what would you like to drink?' Bipin Patel asked Sheena, not me.

'Black coffees would be fine, thank you.'

Poppy Flowers was now on Bipin Patel's desk, flattened out with four small paperweights that kept it from rolling back. They were silver paperweights, which made me wonder if the pretentious prick had specifically got them for the purpose.

'Do you have any more of these in your locker?' I jested, looking at the large safe on the left of his desk. It was a two-foot by two-foot safe, cemented into the concrete wall, so it was difficult to estimate its depth. All that was visible was its door; Bipin Patel had been clever enough to take the painting out and lock the safe before we were taken into his ostentatious office. It was metal: steel or titanium, but it did not worry me. I didn't anticipate breaking the metal door in any event. As Bipin admired Sheena, I stole glances at the locker. It had a heavy locking arm, a touch-sensitive numeric pad, a keyhole, and no insignia to indicate which company had made it, which, in my experience was what most people who needed lockers wanted. Giving away the name of the company that manufactured it also gave away information about its strength and methods of breaking into it. Someone, somewhere in the world might have cracked open a similar safe and uploaded a video of the process on YouTube.

I glanced casually around and noticed that there were two CCTV cameras in the room: one facing the locker, the other facing the only door in the office. I realised that when I came here after hours, I'd have to be in disguise, and not be the professor who was visiting him now. I looked around to see if the place was alarmed, but I couldn't see anything.

Nevertheless, I knew enough to have realized that just because there were no outward signs, it didn't mean that the place wasn't secured. And maybe the outer space of the office had an alarm, too, to avoid an intruder even getting close to the locker.

'You are insatiable, Professor,' Bipin Patel retorted at my inquisitiveness about other paintings in his collection. 'No, this is the only piece I have that's worth putting in there.' He gestured at the locker.

'Lovely, Mr Patel,' Sheena hadn't looked up from the painting since it had been rolled out.

'But is it genuine, that is the question. That's what I'd like you to tell me, Professor.'

I took out a tan leather pouch from my pocket: a faux antique. It had to look worn out, like something I'd been using for years and not bought only a few days ago off a random website. I extracted the lens from it like a pro and held it near the painting in front of me. I could feel two pairs of eyes drilling holes in the back of my head as I bent over and brought my head down for a close examination. I felt icy sweat sliding down my spine.

The canvas looked old and distressed, so it wasn't painted a few weeks or months or a couple of years ago, that was for sure. And that was it – that was the absolute extent of my superficial knowledge. But what I had was intelligence gathered by Udhham Kumar and the Japanese buyer, and their list of possible people who could have the original *Poppy Flowers* included Bipin Patel. Putting those facts together wasn't rocket science, just common sense.

But what I didn't know was whether Bipin Patel had kept the original someplace else and was showing me a counterfeit to catch me out. I brought my face closer and breathed in to check if I could catch the lingering fumes of ethanol or any other spirit to clear an old canvas to get this painted over. Nope. The colours looked moderately faded like any painting of the same age if they weren't preserved by desiccant dehumidifiers that were typically deployed in museums. The hues appeared quite like I had imagined; in fact, a lot better than I had imagined. If this was not Van Gogh's work, then it had to be a contemporary of Van Gogh's who had painted this, which didn't make sense whatsoever. Who would have known then that Vincent van Gogh would become so famous that his work would be sold for the sum we were talking about? Why would anyone have painted a replica of his work back in the nineteenth century?

'It is an original,' I declared. 'But that is merely my assessment. If you want a confirmation, it needs to be sent for professional testing.'

'Thanks. Your confirmation is enough. I have no desire to parade it around and let the world know I own this. I've always been certain it's genuine, but your word has put my mind at rest.'

'Why do you want to hide this gem, Mr Patel? It is so beautiful; it should be displayed and admired. You have no idea how many art enthusiasts would love to see it…'

If Sheena was trying to change Bipin Patel's mind, she was wasting her minty breath. She was missing the whole point. The moment Bipin Patel put this painting on the wall and opened the door to let people come and admire it, the authorities would ask him to surrender it. It was stolen property. It didn't matter how much he had paid for it, it still remained stolen property. And it rightfully belonged to the Mohamed Mahmoud Khalil Museum in Giza.

'I don't want publicity, Sheena.'

How magnanimous, what a gentleman! I wanted to laugh. Bipin Patel, from what I knew, was a man without a soul. He'd sell his son for a profit if he could. This humble stance did not suit him.

'Could I take a picture of it, if you don't mind, please?' I asked.

'But there are far better photographs of it already on the web, Professor Rueben.'

'I know, but for me to see the original with my eyes, it means so much ...' I pleaded like my life depended on it.

'Okay, but no flash,' he said, clearly uneasy but unable to refuse something apparently so small to someone who had just done him such a huge favour.

'Of course not.'

I took out my BlackBerry and took a shot.

'Could I take one too, please?'

I saw Bipin Patel's eyes move from me to Sheena. And it was the moment I had anticipated; if I asked for a picture, Sheena would too, I knew. I tilted my phone and clicked a picture of the locked safe. Bipin Patel had been correct. The pictures of *Poppy Flowers* on the web were far superior than anyone could ever click with a camera phone. As Sheena shot her picture, I attached the picture of the safe, then realised there was no mobile signal here for me to forward it to my friend. Strange. No mobile signal in the heart of Delhi? Then it struck me. The office had jammers cutting off the mobile signal. Anyway, I deleted the picture of the safe and let it go from the main folder. I could always retrieve it later. I did that because I was certain Bipin Patel might want to have a look at the pictures we had snapped, and he did.

We chatted about other stuff for a while. A few more paintings and pieces of art were discussed. We exchanged numbers, and promised to keep in touch before we left his office. Sheena chatted away excitedly, but I tuned her out as I focussed on our exit route. There was a camera facing the elevator door. There was one camera in the elevator as we travelled down six floors. There was another one at the main entrance into the building, which wasn't in the front facing the road, but on the side. And there was a watchman; I presumed there'd be one at night as well, but this one, right now, wasn't armed. In fact, he looked like he had retired from someplace else and was merely here to supplement his pension.

Outside, the sun was weak and the air was still as Sheena and I walked to her car. As I had travelled here with her, she naturally expected me to get into the car with her so she could drop me back. And although I wanted to stay put, hang around in the area to check out the nocturnal security arrangements around the building, and also record the time Bipin Patel's office got vacant, I decided that might send out the wrong signal. The smart thing to do was to hitch a ride home with my beautiful companion and then drive back a little later.

12
THE CAPTAIN'S STORY

A Week Later:

'I knew it,' exclaimed Udhham Kumar. 'I knew only *you* could have done it.' I could imagine Udhham Kumar jumping on a trampoline with happiness when I told him that I knew where the painting was.

'I told you I'd get to it without anyone knowing what we were after.'

'How does it look?'

'It's simply amazing.' That's as much as I could give him. After all, me attempting to describe colours and pigments to Udhham Kumar would be akin to the blind leading the blind.

'So what now? How do we get it?' He got to the point.

'I have recced the area over a couple of days and nights and found out everything I could. But I'll need some more time. At any rate, I need to buy some equipment to break into the vault. It's cemented into the wall—'

'You're not going in alone,' Udhham said.

'What do you mean, I'm "not going in alone"?'

'It's too risky.'

'For whom? It's me at the frontline, and that was our arrangement, Udhham...'

'I've changed my mind. I know it's you who will bear the consequences if you're caught, but it's me who will lose the painting, and I cannot afford that. And even from your perspective, you should have someone guarding your back, don't you think?'

'I guess it doesn't matter what I think if you've already made up your mind, but if you send someone and things go wrong, I am not to be blamed.'

'What do you mean by "if things go wrong"?'

'Well, it's not simple for even one person to slip into an office complex undetected, and you want two to go in … it just doubles the risk.'

'Three. I want two people to accompany you.'

'You're shitting me!'

'Nope. I think you'll appreciate what I'm doing here. Safeguarding you,' he said, all generosity and concern.

For a moment, I wondered how stupid I looked for this man to think I was buying his warped explanation? Was I to think that Udhham Kumar was worried about my safety and welfare? It was apparent that he didn't trust me. Well, 200 million US dollars were a good enough reason not to trust your own flesh-and-blood.

'Who would be the two people accompanying me?'

'Damodar, whom you've already met, and one more person. They'll be reaching your Hauz Khas residence tomorrow evening.'

'Make sure you tell them who's leading the heist. There should be no confusion on that front or we'd unnecessarily waste time in establishing hierarchies.'

'Oh, there's no confusion in my mind, Captain. You will be the leader of the pack. I'll make sure that they know and accept that.'

'Good. Thanks.'

'It's Tuesday today. Should we aim for you three to go in Thursday night then?' he asked.

'No. I'd rather carry everything out over the weekend, since that should give us a few days before Bipin Patel discovers that the painting has been taken. I've made certain that he doesn't come to this office on weekends.'

'Sounds good. Okay, I'll leave you to it. My team will be over to meet you tomorrow. Let me know if you need something, and keep me updated.'

'Most definitely.'

Udhham Kumar was confident he had dealt with the situation decisively, not letting his final plan or any apprehension slip through during his call with the Captain.

He dialled Sylvia's number now. 'The time has come,' he said to her.

'I told you he was up to something when I saw him at Barakhamba Road last week with his lady friend, and then, after she dropped him home, he drove back, parked and scouted around on foot for a couple of hours. And subsequently, he's been going back to reconnoitre the same building almost every night. That was a sure giveaway.'

'So he isn't as smart as he thinks he is. He didn't realise that he was being watched.'

'It isn't that he is not smart, Mr Kumar. It's just that I'm better.' Sylvia chuckled.

'Certainly. My fault for not acknowledging that. You *are* smart.'

'But I also know what he's planning so I had an advantage. What do we do now?' she asked.

'I've told him that Damodar and another person – you – will be joining him at his residence tomorrow evening. You three need to work together; the Captain will lead the mission, but only until you have the painting in your hands. Then Damodar and you take the lead. Once you guys are out, you call me and drive out of Delhi. Do not waste a single minute. You drive and Damodar will guide. He knows the route to follow to avoid police checkpoints.'

'And the Captain? Does he come with us?'

'Yes, but not all the way. Damodar will take a diversion, and at one point, my guys will be waiting. They'll take care of the Captain – finish him and bury him there and then. As I told you, I can't afford to leave a loose end, and after this heist, the Captain will be one. His job is to get the painting for me, and as soon as that's done, his part in our story is over.'

'So you save his fee?'

'I hope you understand that I'm not doing this for money; it's more a safety issue. If I gave him the money, what's the guarantee he won't come back asking for more, and try to blackmail me? At any rate, I've earmarked that money for you and Damodar, which is over and above the money I promised you for this job. In fact, you and I can travel to Tokyo together to see Mr Haruhiko Sakai—'

'Who's that?'

'Mr Haruhiko Sakai is the art collector who's buying the painting.'

'Oh, I see. Well, thank you, Mr Kumar.'

'I look after my own, Sylvia.'

'It's good to know that,' she said, and hung up.

Udhham could sense that Sylvia was impressed with him and his proposal. Smiling to himself, he called Damodar in.

Udhham Kumar knew that Damodar didn't like the Captain. He also knew that Damodar was a wild card. He was built like a small mountain and had a violent temperament. But if Udhham trusted anyone more than he trusted even Sylvia, it was Damodar. He was concerned that, despite skills, Sylvia could fall short in taking the Captain out. He couldn't risk sending her alone for a face-to-face encounter. What if a confrontation occurred? No, she would certainly not be enough. Damodar, on the other hand, was more than enough.

'There is no need for him to lead us to the painting, boss, if you tell me where it is, I'll get it for you all by myself. I don't need an assistant,' Damodar responded when Udhham told him of his plan.

'Damodar, this isn't all about muscle, it's also about tact. The Captain knows what he's doing, so it's best we let him guide us till he gets us the painting. Once you have that, you know what to do,' Udhham explained.

'As you say, but tell him not to order me around or I'll twist his neck a hundred and eighty degrees.'

'That will not do. You have to maintain a very calm front, Damodar. Nothing in your countenance should make the Captain suspicious. He should willingly travel back with you.'

'Okay, boss, but why do I need to carry that floozy with me?'

'Don't ever call her that again, Damodar.' Udhham didn't raise his voice, but there was steel in it.

'I'm sorry, Udhham bhai. Never again, I promise.' Damodar was immediately contrite.

'The reason I want you and Sylvia both on the job is because the Captain is too cunning. Sylvia will be of great help if he decides to be uncooperative. And on your way, if you come across a police check-post, having a woman with you will make things look less suspicious.'

'I got it, boss. Not a problem.'

'Sylvia will be there to pick you up from the railway station tomorrow. Here's her number,' Udhham said, handing the other man a piece of paper. 'Both of you will go to the Captain's house tomorrow evening and camp there until the job's done.'

'Yes, bhai.'

'One more thing ...' He paused and swallowed. 'Do not come back here without the painting and Sylvia. I want them both.'

'Yes, bhai. Don't worry.'

'Now let's have a drink. We need to go over the details of the plan once, before you leave for Delhi.'

Drinks were Old Monk and Coca Cola.

'Okay, when you get out of the building with the painting, you take control of the entire operation. Sylvia should drive, and you ensure that the Captain sits in the front and you sit behind him. Drive out of Delhi directly from Barakhamba Road towards Haryana, not UP. If the Captain asks why, tell him you don't want anyone linking you to our state. Drive to Palwal – it is approximately sixty-odd kilometres away from Barakhamba. If the police flag you down, let Sylvia talk to them. You should resist any contact with the police. And remember, no violence whatsoever.'

Damodar took a sip from his glass and nodded.

'At Palwal, do not take the Yamuna Expressway towards Agra – take the Aligarh route instead. Again, if the Captain asks why, tell him you have information that the expressway might have police blockades; that should keep any suspicion at bay. But do not explain anything if not asked, as that might raise doubts. Okay?'

'Yes, boss.'

'Then cross the border, and about forty kilometres down the Palwal-Aligarh road, you'll find a small place called Jattari. Keep an eye out for the signposts so you don't miss it. Our guys will put up a blockade – they'll be in uniform, pseudo police, but it will be too late for the Captain to react by the time you are close enough to discern that. Hand the Captain over to them – I don't care, dead or alive – and they'll take care of him. Then Sylvia and you continue to Deoria. I'll be here.'

'You've planned it all,' Damodar said, admiration clear in his voice.

'Damodar, I trust you. You have almost eight hundred kilometres to cover from Jattari to Deoria with Sylvia alone. You guys will need a few hours of rest, so make a stop somewhere safe, but don't do anything that you might regret later. Treat Sylvia with utmost respect, do you understand?' His meaning was clear, and Damodar nodded gravely.

'Yes, bhai, you can trust me.'

'Thank you, Damodar. Go get the painting and Sylvia tomorrow and I'll reward you with more money than you can ever spend in your lifetime.'

If the police of any country had unlimited time and resources, all criminals would be brought to book and there would be no unresolved cases or miscarriages of justice. But they too, like all other government departments, have finite resources. They simply cannot afford to follow up every pointer. Not to forget, there are always other limitations halting sincere progress – the backbreaking bureaucracy, people's personal agendas, pressures from those higher up the ladder.

But perhaps it was because of how low he was on that ladder that Sub-inspector Hari Mohan Gupta had all the time in the world, and no one preventing him from pursuing his single-minded agenda. Most of his old contacts had been more than happy to indulge him. It took him a while and some travel, but he eventually traced the Captain's steps – from Pushkar to Benares to Gorakhpur to the covert meeting with Udhham Kumar at his remote countryside mansion in Deoria.

And then, finally, back to Delhi.

Something was cooking between Udhham Kumar and the Captain. Hari Mohan didn't know what it was, but he knew that it had needed the Captain to pose as an art professor in a college. From a con artist to a sanyasi to a professor – Hari Mohan was intrigued, and amused. And while he didn't have the details yet, he was bright enough to grasp the basics – Udhham Kumar wanted a piece of art, and had hired the Captain's services to procure it.

He arrived at the College of Art in Delhi Technological University on Thursday, only to be informed that Professor Rueben was on leave for a few days and would only return to work on Monday. Since Hari Mohan was carrying out the investigation in his individual capacity, he couldn't officially convince the authorities to part with the professor's residential address. Moreover, he didn't want anyone getting suspicious and warning the cheat. He reckoned that four days wouldn't make much of a difference.

How was he to know that Professor Albert Rueben would never return to the college?

13

THE CAPTAIN'S STORY

My Blackberry pinged. The message read – 'Change of plan…'

If Udhham Kumar had thought I wasn't aware that my house and my car were wired, he had missed the mark by a mile. Calling from my home using either mobile or landline meant the surveillance would pick up the conversation. There had to be some real change in plan if I was supposed to step out to make the call, as it had never been required since I started here.

The good news was that I made that call.

The bad news was I had limited time between now and the next evening to procure all the equipment I needed.

You'd have thought once I had the painting in my hands, the job was almost over, but the game, I sensed, would begin only after the painting had been recovered from Bipin Patel's locker. The stakes had been raised now, and my gut told me it would soon turn ugly. To say I wasn't a bit anxious would be a lie. Everyone experiences fear at some point in life. No one is always totally fearless. Fear is natural. It is good. It provides positive energy to do something one fears; the trick is to not let it transform into panic.

I retrieved the weapons I had saved earlier. Two Glocks and two Heckler & Koch MP5s. Both Glocks were 17s, and they were fully loaded with two magazines to spare. Sixty-eight bullets in total, more than enough to shoot thirty-four people, even with a 50 percent hit rate, and mine was certainly better than that. A handgun, for all the glamorisation in films and fiction, is a highly unreliable weapon – the thumb-rule is that the longer the barrel of the gun, the straighter it shoots. Ideally, the shooter should be adroit or the target should be as close as twenty to thirty feet. But there was little chance of encountering too many adversaries at that range. My worry was the H&K. The 9×19 mm Parabellum cartridges used by H&K aren't as high powered as I would have liked. And I had no spare magazines for them. But I rationalised that it wasn't the weapon that counted in the end, it was the quickness of the finger. A small underpowered car could beat a Ferrari if its driver had bigger balls.

The fact that the heist was on Friday afforded me the luxury of time. If all went to plan – if the alarms didn't go off, if no one was shot and the break in wasn't reported until later – the earliest Bipin Patel would find out about the robbery would be on Monday morning. By that time, it would already be too late. We'd be out of his office and out of Delhi, and he'd have to live with it. What else could he do? Report an illegitimate piece of art stolen, one that he had himself unscrupulously acquired?

I had procured the correct sized tube for the painting, exactly the same size I had seen at Bipin Patel's office –

twenty-two inches long, with a half-inch margin on both sides. I needed to prepare to hide the painting on me, if things went wrong and we had to escape on foot. I took the hard tube I bought, put it firmly against my spine, right below the shirt collar, to below the lumbar curve, where it sat in my boxers, and fastened it firmly using Velcro belts on the top and bottom. It was a bit uncomfortable at first, but like all other things in life, after a few hours, even the tube rubbing on my ass became a part of me. I kept the shirt out and wore a cotton jacket on top – which I needed anyway, to conceal a handgun in its holster – and the slight tubular shape was concealed. I practised sitting, standing and walking with it strapped on.

I had told the college that I was going out of town during my leave, and made sure that Sheena knew about it too. I didn't want her dropping by to check in on me for some frivolous reason and catching me with Udhham's team.

I didn't know the exact time Udhham's people would arrive, only that they were coming sometime in the evening. But evening could be as early as four, and what if they turned up at three? I removed the spare tyre from my car and filled the empty space with a bag that contained the ammunition and some clothes, masks and other accoutrements like wigs, etc., for the disguises. I didn't know what would be required, and whether we would even get time to change, but it was best to carry what I could as I wasn't coming back to this house.

I had a bottle of Bulleit in the house. I had a shot of it and chased it down with a Kingfisher. Three shots and three beers later, I made myself a masala omelette with green chillies and wolfed it down.

14

Damodar Yadav was dumbstruck when he saw Sylvia. He had seen her from a distance before, and had known that she was gorgeous, but being this close to her in the backseat of a cab was an entirely different experience. The fragrance of her body – the lotion, the shampoo, whatever – filled his nostrils and emptied his brain. He remembered his promise to his boss, but couldn't help stealing glances at the woman next to him. His allegiance to Udhham bhai was because the bhai had money, and money made him the boss. And wasn't Damodar here to earn even more money for bhai? 200 million dollars to be specific.

But Sylvia? She was just like Damodar – just another employee. Udhham Kumar was using both of them as pawns in this game. If anything went wrong, it was their necks on the line. What did that wealthy Udhham Kumar have to lose? Money, of course, but there was no mortal threat to him, whereas a million things could go wrong for Damodar and Sylvia between now and when they carried the painting back to their boss. Agreed, Udhham Kumar had promised Damodar a reward far better than he had ever dreamt of, but how much was that, really? And what was the guarantee that the bastard wouldn't finish Damodar off like he planned to do with the Captain? He was as expendable as the Captain. The more he thought, the angrier he became. Suddenly, the prospect of being a loyal servant to a third-rate politician for the rest of his life felt depressing.

'You okay?' asked Sylvia, looking at Damodar.

'Yes … oh yes … I was just thinking …' It was too soon to confide in her. They'd only just met for the first time, and Damodar was aware that Sylvia had known Udhham for ages. He didn't know for sure, but he guessed that it had been some paid-for encounter that had begun their association. But the fact that they had stayed in touch for so long meant that there was a deeper relationship between them. And Udhham had made it clear to Damodar that he wanted both Sylvia and the painting. He couldn't discern if he could break her commitment towards Udhham. What if she told Udhham Kumar what Damodar was thinking? He couldn't take that risk. But if Sylvia didn't join him in what he was beginning to plan, he would be pitted against two opponents. Not good.

The fact was, the more Damodar Yadav thought about it, the more he reckoned that *he* deserved the painting, and the money from its sale. Initially, the thought felt foreign, even alien, but the more time he spent on the idea, the stronger it grew. Yes, the painting belonged to *him*.

But how would he make sure it came to him? There seemed to be only one way – killing both Sylvia and the Captain. But he knew he needed to be careful. As per the plan, Sylvia was to call Udhham Kumar immediately after acquiring the painting. If anything happened to her, and she didn't make that call, Udhham would know something had gone wrong. And if she did make the call but then the three of them didn't show up in Jattari, as per schedule, that would raise a red flag too. All things considered, he couldn't get rid of Sylvia until they dumped the Captain. Once the Captain was taken care of, news of the same would travel from Udhham's boys to their master and he and Sylvia would be on their way, with an over ten-hour long drive ahead of them. And it's these ten hours that Damodar could use. He could offer her half the loot and try to buy her loyalty. And he knew that he needed her. He had no idea how he'd sell the painting after he got it, and acknowledged Sylvia would be better able to manage that. It would be best if she agreed. Both for him and her. Alone with him in the car or in a hotel room, she wouldn't be able to hoodwink him. If she agreed, well and good. If she didn't, he'd just have to get rid of her and find another way to sell that painting.

Plan B, in that case would be to hide the painting and call and trade with Udhham Kumar on Damodar's terms – a fifty-fifty deal, like an equal partner and not some inferior henchman.

He was still lost, daydreaming and planning, when their cab arrived at Hauz Khas.

Damodar checked out the Captain once again. The man was about four inches shorter and maybe forty kilos lighter than him. His handshake was firm enough for Damodar to gauge that the muscles in the arm attached to it were toned. He wouldn't be an easy opponent, but wasn't too forbidding either. His house had three bedrooms, all on the ground floor, and Sylvia picked first.

Sylvia and Damodar returned from their rooms after freshening up, and the three of them met at the dining table to discuss the plan. There was a bottle of Bulleit, three quarters full, kept with glasses and an ice bucket. The Captain poured a shot each for all three.

'The fifth floor of the building where Bipin Patel's office is, is not fully occupied at the moment. A small portion on the rear side was vacated a few months back and the new tenants haven't moved in. I have been there and have left a few tools in the storage space above the toilets ...' the Captain explained. He also told them that he had checked out and made sure that the place wasn't fitted with an alarm system, which made sense, since there was nothing inside except some old furniture.

As per the plan, the three of them would go into the building separately on Friday, all of them in disguises and pretending to visit different offices. Visitors to the building were only required to pencil in their names and addresses in a register kept at the entrance. No one verified or asked for ID. No one gave visitors a lanyard with a coded tag to tally the entries and exits at the end of the day. Most people left the building without signing the register, so it was impossible that the watchman would notice any of them going in and not returning. There were no metal detectors at the entrance, so they could get in without any alarming beeps. The Captain confirmed that he'd already made the key for the empty, deserted office on the fifth floor. They could slip in anytime during the day but should definitely get there before 5 p.m., since that was when the office crowd finished work and a lot of people were on the move; it would be better to avoid being in the corridors at that time so that no one remembered them later. Once in the fifth-floor safe house, no one was to switch on any lights or make any noise.

They'd go there in one car – the Captain's Audi. The tank was full. It would be parked in the parking lot of a hotel opposite Patel's building. The Captain explained that this would be less risky than parking in the building's own lot, since they would get there before offices closed, and their car might get clocked by some office worker on their return. Also, there was an ATM on the ground floor of the building and a guard was always stationed outside it. When most of the office crowd left for the day, their car might become conspicuous to him, being the only one left there. They didn't know how long they'd need to use the same car, as the distance from Delhi to Deoria was almost nine hundred kilometres. It was best to play it safe and not leave any clues behind to help the police or Bipin Patel's men, in the event that the robbery was found out before they were safely out of the city.

They would exit the building together after the heist. Just in case the night watchman raised an alarm, it would be best to handle the situation as a team.

'Although I suspect Bipin Patel would be reporting the theft before we leave town, nothing should get traced back to us or to this property, I think we should wash everything we use in the house.' The Captain pointed to the whiskey tumblers.

'Now, let's order some pizza, and then it's best that you both sleep over the plan and think about what I may have missed. Remember, we are a team, we have the same goal,' the Captain said.

Everyone acknowledged that with a nod and a smile. Before wrapping up, they decided that while it would be impossible to remove the Captain's fingerprints from the house completely, the other two would throw away their own belongings on the way if they didn't need them. In case of someone tracing the crime back to the Captain, the house would be searched, and they needed to leave behind as few clues as possible.

For dinner, the Captain had been cautious and ordered three pizzas from three different shops. He didn't want to raise the curiosity levels of the delivery boys, who had so far only been delivering food enough for one person to the house.

After they'd eaten, everyone retired to their respective bedrooms. Damodar lay in his bed and wondered if he was making a mistake in picking Sylvia as an ally. Perhaps it would be better if he tried to convince the Captain to switch sides. If he and the Captain joined hands, there was little that Sylvia could do except report them to Udhham. The more he thought about it, the more it seemed like the Captain would make a better partner. For one, the man didn't have the kind of long relationship with Udhham Kumar that Sylvia had. And furthermore, he seemed like a stronger, more meticulous ally – Damodar couldn't spot a single flaw in the entire plan the Captain had outlined for them. And lastly, the two of them together could take on a good four to five men simultaneously.

He twisted and turned in his bed, and then figured that he didn't have to take a decision just then. And anyway, he wanted to run through the pros and cons and the possible consequences in his mind properly before he decided if he wanted a partner at all, or would rather go solo.

15

Thursday

Jattari, Uttar Pradesh

A Tata 407 with three men drove eastwards from Jattari early in the morning. They had started the previous day from Deoria, driven to Jattari and had slept in a cheap hotel near the bus stop. They had their work cut out for them, and knew exactly what they were supposed to do over the next three days. Aamir, Sukhiya and Pundit were Udhham Kumar's henchmen. With them, they carried spades, shovels, forks, hoes and metal pans to shift the soil and gravel they'd dig up. The truck was also loaded with drums and bars and light-reflecting cones to create a fake police barrier to stop traffic. Their target – a black Audi A4 with three passengers – one woman and two men – was due to arrive Saturday morning, but their orders had been to prepare everything and to be ready by the midnight before that. They also carried a small tent that they would stay in until their job was done.

Before leaving Deoria, they had received a stern warning from Udhham Kumar – failure would not be tolerated. If they did not accomplish what they had been sent for, their wives and children back in Deoria would be tortured and killed.

A few kilometres southeast of Jattari, on the 22A Palwal-Aligarh Road, population and businesses became scarce, and then disappeared altogether for a few kilometres before a small locality started to emerge again. The three men got off the tarmac, turned left and drove for a few hundred metres until they found an area that had a cluster of trees dense enough to park the truck behind. Aamir walked back to the main road to check and confirm that their vehicle wasn't visible to passing traffic unless someone stopped and specifically looked for it. Out came the tools and the three men started digging a pit. It was hard land that had baked for months under the summer sun, and they had to dig a three feet deep, seven feet long and two feet wide cavity; the trio laboured on until the sun set for the day. Sukhiya drove back to Jattari for supplies of food, water and cheap rum. The other two put up a little tent behind the truck. They drank until eleven in the evening, ate and slept, only to start all over again at sunrise.

The grave was finally ready by Friday afternoon. They parked their truck right over the cavity and rested for a few hours; they knew they needed to save their energy for the night.

The intended occupant of the grave could arrive anytime in the early hours of Saturday morning.

16

Thursday

New Delhi

His mind in turmoil, Damodar had a restless night and woke up before sunrise. He'd spent the night weighing the pros and cons of picking either the Captain or Sylvia as an ally, and eventually zeroed in on Sylvia. His decision was based on the least amount of threat posed and not on her intrinsic worth. She would be a lot easier to overpower should something go wrong after they got rid of the Captain.

He had also decided to speak to her now, and not leave it for after they crossed Jattari. If something went wrong at the time of the heist, if the Captain pulled something, they could then act as a team against him. All Damodar needed was an hour alone with Sylvia.

The opportunity presented itself after breakfast.

'I need to go out,' the Captain said.

'What for?' asked Sylvia.

'I need to buy some supplies and I think I should pick up some microwavable food for us.'

'We'll come with you.'

'I don't think that's a good idea.'

'Why not?'

'You both have just arrived in Delhi, no one has seen you … more importantly, no one has seen the three of us together. Let's keep it that way.'

'The Captain has a point,' Damodar agreed, seeing his chance for a one-on-one with Sylvia.

'Okay, fair enough,' she said.

'I need to speak with you,' Damodar said as soon as the door closed behind the Captain.

'What about?'

'The plan. And Udhham bhai.'

'Go on, then. Is something wrong?' she asked.

'Well, not really, but I have my own fears now …' he replied.

'What do you mean?'

'If Udhham can decide to have the Captain killed after the job, don't you think he could do the same to us? We only know as much as he's told us, right? What if his men at Jattari are instructed to kill the two of us too? Who knows how many graves they are digging as we speak?'

He could see her mind working, weighing his words and their implication. He saw emotions flit across her face – suspicion, danger, fear, rage.

'Think about it, Sylvia, I've heard him say enough times that the painting is worth some 200 million dollars. That's a lot of money,' he pressed on. He outlined his alternative plan, the one he had been working on for the past couple of days. Take the painting, get rid of the Captain, disappear from Udhham Kumar's radar, then sell the painting and share the proceeds, just the two of them.

'He won't ever stop looking for us,' Sylvia said, her brow furrowed. 'We'll be making a lifelong enemy of him.'

So she was considering his proposal, Damodar thought, breathing a little easier.

'We can work on that, but first, are you in?' he pressed.

'I don't trust you,' she said flatly.

'Why not?' But he had anticipated this question. After all, Sylvia knew that Damodar had worked for Udhham Kumar for years. Anyone in her place would have also had misgivings, and thought that he was doing this to check her allegiance to their boss.

'I understand, Syvia, but don't you see that I am taking the same risk as you? If you report what I've proposed just now back to Udhham Kumar, I'm a dead man,' Damodar reasoned.

'What I don't understand is, why do you need me? You could do this alone,' Sylvia said.

'I could, but two heads are better than one. If we are a team, we'd have more control, especially if the Captain doesn't play ball – two on one is better than three of us working independently against each other, don't you think?'

They discussed Damodar's suggestion some more and slowly, he could see her coming around to the plan.

'There's one thing …' she said finally. 'If we are in this together; that is, eliminating Udhham Kumar from the equation, then we are not driving to Jattari at all.'

'Why not?' he asked, although he'd had the same concern since the morning.

'Honestly, once we get to Jattari, we are in Udhham's territory, we are in his men's claws. If you know him, you'd know he might have changed the plan and not mentioned it to us. What if we get there and his men take the painting away from us, and leave us with nothing? Worse still, what if they have been told, like you suggested earlier, to eliminate all three of us?'

'You're right. So what do you suggest?'

'We need to get rid of the Captain before we get to Jattari. I'd rather we skip town as soon as we have the painting. We take the Captain out, and we race to Mumbai.'

'We could do that. But once we get to Mumbai, how do we find a buyer for the painting?'

'We don't find *a* buyer; we get in touch with *the* buyer, the Japanese man who was in touch with Udhham.'

'You know him?'

'I don't know him, but I know his name; it shouldn't be impossible to find him. How many people of the same name in Japan could be billionaires and art collectors?' Sylvia asked. Damodar noticed that she didn't actually reveal the name of the buyer to him. Clever woman.

Now all they needed was to figure out how, when and where to get rid of the Captain. They talked for another hour and decided on a plan of action, just before the Captain returned.

17

Friday

Deoria, Uttar Pradesh

It was an impromptu decision. When Udhham Kumar had gone to bed the night before, he had no plans of spending his weekend on the road, but who could blame him for the raging butterflies when he was about to make more money in a single transaction than he had made in his entire life to date. 200 million dollars! That was enough to make him give sleep, thirst, hunger, and even sex a wide berth.

It had begun to fall into place over a year ago, when he had attended a two-day seminar on rural development. A Japanese delegation had given a presentation to government officials on efficiently storing and using rainwater for farming. One of the delegates from Japan was Mr Haruhiko Sakai, a billionaire art collector. Over drinks, the tycoon had casually mentioned Van Gogh's *Poppy Flowers*, and how his research had revealed that the painting was in India. Mr Sakai – loosened up after a few drinks – had been blunt about his desire to possess that painting at any cost.

Subsequently, Udhham Kumar met his new Japanese friend in Lucknow. The painting was discussed in more detail – its provenance, its chequered history, its value, and the price Sakai was willing to pay for it. It was apparent that money was no issue for the man. He didn't want to dwell on the morality of procuring it for his collection either. Udhham offered to help, and the deal was struck. Mr Sakai was emphatic about only one thing – he wanted to play no part in the acquisition of the painting. He'd pay once he received the painting and after his experts verified that it was the genuine thing. Any unwarranted fallout, any associated culpability was to be made good or taken care of by Udhham.

A year, Udhham ruminated, and now it would all be over in just a couple of days.

But as the moment drew closer, he suddenly wanted to play an active part in the thing and not just passively sit and wait for the painting to arrive in Deoria.

In such situations, the only person he usually depended on was Damodar – his best driver, but that did not mean he couldn't travel without him. Udhham Kumar told one of the other drivers and two of his security men to drive him to Jattari. He'd take delivery of his treasure personally and travel back with Sylvia and Van Gogh.

18

THE CAPTAIN'S STORY

Friday

New Delhi

It was raining lightly when I woke up on Friday morning – a welcome relief after the scorching heat of Delhi summer. My mother used to say that rain was a good omen. However, every micro-locality has its own theory about rain. Some consider it auspicious; others say it brings bad luck. Scientifically, it's just precipitation, nothing else.

Soon after me, Damodar woke up and emerged from his room. He looked tired, and it didn't require engaging Einstein to work out why. I had heard someone walking in the common area the past two nights and had presumed it was him. Maybe he had a sleeping disorder; maybe the task ahead was making him nervous. Either way, as long as he didn't go to sleep when we were in Bipin Patel's office, it was fine by me.

We had decided to go to Barakhamba Road after lunch. There was little point in getting there in the morning and then having to wait until everyone finished work and left. Damodar insisted on Sylvia driving to the venue. He gave us some moonshine about it being lucky if a woman steered us to a treasure. Total bullshit, but I didn't see any reason to challenge his theory. We drove into the parking area of The Hind hotel on Barakhamba Road. My experience was that hotel parking was generally a safe zone. With guests arriving and leaving all the time, no one particular car raised suspicion if it was parked for too long. We parked, and went in our different directions. We had already exchanged mobile numbers, but our phones were to be kept on silent mode and used only if necessary. If you made or received calls from a mobile phone, the location of the phone, at that particular time, could be retrospectively tracked if someone knew the number. If you did not make the call, the phone's location could not be traced later; they could only pinpoint the phone's whereabouts through active signal triangulation if they were already monitoring you.

Damodar was supposed to be first into the building, followed by Sylvia and then me, which gave me almost two to three hours to pass in the vicinity. I walked out of the hotel, turned right and walked to Janpath. I went straight to Depaul's and ordered a cheese sandwich and a cold coffee. Always eat when you get a chance. Who knew when and where our next morsel would come from? I also got sandwiches and drinks for all of us packed.

I did not look anything like Professor Albert Reuben now. I had had my hair cut short and dyed black, the studious glasses were gone, contact lenses made my eyes camel coloured, and a full, trimmed beard covered the majority of my face. Bipin Patel had obviously not seen Damodar or Sylvia, so they didn't need disguises at the moment. We couldn't avoid the cameras at the entrance of the building or in the elevator car, and part of the plan was – once we were all in the building – I would be the one to get to Bipin's office on the eighth floor and cover the cameras in his office, and so, it'd only be me on the cameras and not my accomplices. I thought about it long and hard, and there was no way I could avoid being on the cameras, but it didn't bother me. I was in disguise, and I wasn't coming anywhere within a hundred-kilometre radius of Bipin Patel once this was over. If and when Bipin Patel started his search and called for the CCTV recordings from the public areas in the building, and made the connection of who else could have been involved in the heist besides a bearded guy, it would already be too late.

I scribbled zigzag lines instead of a name on the register when I entered the building a little after four. I walked in purposefully, took the elevator directly to the fifth floor, and went straight to the office where we were meant to gather, opening it with the key I had made on previous visits and proceeded to check on the tools I had hidden there. Damodar and Sylvia were already in. They thanked me when I told them that I had brought in some refreshments for them. In the next hour, the building slowly emptied out as employees from various offices began leaving for the day. The noise and chatter outside reduced around 6.30 p.m., and virtually petered out by 8 p.m. But we needed to be certain that the building was completely empty before stepping out, and chances were, a few dedicated workaholics were still there somewhere, so we agreed we wouldn't rush into things that we might regret later. Passing time was a chore, with little to talk amongst ourselves besides the plan that we had recapped twice already since we had been there.

I had seen their silhouettes and knew that Damodar and Sylvia were both carrying handguns. And I was sure that they had figured out that I was carrying one too.

We waited until 11 p.m., and then it was time to take our next step.

I picked up the large bag of tools and walked out. The others would follow me after five minutes. Even if the elevators were operational, we wouldn't be using them. The noise, in the silence of the night, would be heard all the way down to the ground floor, where the watchman stood guard.

I knew where the staircase was, and the door to it was luckily unlocked, which saved me some time. Three floors up though, the door opening into the foyer of the eighth floor was secured by a standard mortise lock, which took me under two minutes to open. It took me another six minutes to cover the first camera that faced the elevator, surpass the lock at the main office reception, walk into Bipin Patel's inner sanctum that contained the locker, breach that lock and cover the two cameras that I had seen inside his office on my visit with brown paper.

Sylvia and Damodar came in a minute later.

'Great work,' Damodar said. 'That was quick, Captain.'

We had previously decided not to switch on the office lights right away. Anything that was a risk, however small, was unnecessary. In a darkened building, what if the night watchman came out for a round and just glanced up, and seeing unexplained light on one of the floors, suspected something and came up to check or dialled 100?

The key lock in Bipin Patel's vault took a fraction over five minutes to crack – I already had a picture of the size and shape of the keyhole, and I had crafted a few keys to work with. But then the touchscreen numeric pad began giving me trouble. It turned out to be harder to crack than I had accounted for. The older ones – both push button and rotary dial – were a lot easier to break into; there used to be a click you heard, if you knew what to expect, and that was a giveaway. The challenge with the new touchscreen numeric ones was that one needed to work with fingerprints. However, most people were smart enough to wipe them off. And even if they didn't, there was no way to predict the sequence. And anyway, Bipin Patel clearly belonged to the smart club. His prints had been wiped off with care. There was no way of guessing the code now, and no time either. Well, I had kept the possibility of this happening in mind and was prepared, though I had hoped it wouldn't come to it.

My research on the vault, based on the picture I had clicked of it, told me that the thickness of its door was between 165 to 175 mm, that it was fire and force resistant, and had up to seven passive front bolts, but no active ones; active bolts could trigger an alarm if forcibly dislodged. While the vault had no brand name or make written on it, I had used the visual likeness between the two-touchscreen numeric keypads and the keyholes to zero in on the model it could be, and the key lock I had just opened with my master key turned out to be eight-levered, just like the one I had researched. That gave me some confidence that I'd managed to find the correct model online.

Knowing that this might happen, two days ago, I had left a power circular saw in the building. Yesterday, when I'd left the house for my errands, I had come back here to leave a heavy-duty power drill with all the attachments for the saw and drill. If it had been any other safe, maybe a bullet would have come in handy, but seven bolts required seven shots, at the very least. Not ideal even if fired with a silencer clamped to the gun. If everything worked, the power saw cutter would need thirty minutes to an hour to cut through the 175 mm metal; we might not even require the drill, but it was best to be prepared. I plugged the saw in while Damodar held the torch up. Sylvia, in the meanwhile, had taped newspaper on the windows, lowered all the blinds in the office and had put Bipin Patel's desk lamp on the floor and switched it on. The light was enough for our purpose and we were certain not much could be seen from eight floors down.

There was a sharp sound when the saw drove into the metal, screeching sparks. But twenty minutes into the job, we knew we could do it, although we realised that we had to revise our timeline. Judging by the progress we had made in twenty minutes, an hour for the whole job was too optimistic. We also needed to switch the motor off every ten minutes to prevent it from overheating, and either Damodar or Sylvia had to walk out into the main foyer to check if anyone had come looking, attracted by the unusual sound despite this being a soundproof room. Considering all the pauses we begrudgingly had to make, we reckoned that the whole thing would take up to four hours. Then again, the execution of any plan was always an exercise in improvisation. Obstacles cropped up on account of factors that you would not have foreseen or calculated. And that was not good. It changed a lot of things. Our delay here could lead to complications. One: much as we were in consensus that it would take up to four hours to cut out the metal sheet to get our hands on the painting, supposing it didn't? And sure, while it was the weekend, and the chances of Bipin Patel or any of his assistants walking into the office were slim, they weren't non-existent. Two: even if someone came in or we didn't finish the job before morning, we couldn't leave now, because the vandalised safe door would tell its story loud enough. And we couldn't continue working the following day, as I was aware that a cleaning crew came in on weekends to attend to the office and the building. Irrespective of which floor was being cleaned, the noise would certainly betray us. The only alternative was to stay inside the room for another twenty-four hours, and if anyone dropped in, there would be bloodshed, which I had so wanted to avoid from the beginning.

It was past 3 a.m. and I had only managed to cut two sides. The safe door being two feet by two feet, the plan had been to cut the front panel through by making incisions that were six inches inwards from all sides so we didn't have to bother about the bolts and hinges that secured the door to the frame; much like a cat flap – only this flap wouldn't dangle from the top, but the square foot piece we'd cut would be taken out altogether to provide access to the contents. My arm ached with the strain, and Damodar took over. I wondered why it hadn't occurred to him to take over the task earlier, considering he was younger and much stronger. It had taken me the best part of four hours to cut two sides and he was already through one side in an hour – a glimmer of hope. We still had a little while before daybreak, and if Damodar took another hour, we'd have the painting out of the vault by five.

4.45 a.m. – two inches left.

We took a mandatory recess. The last thing any of us wanted was to come so close and then have the power saw flaming up or breaking down.

I strolled out to check and there was no one anywhere on the floor, but to my dismay, the predawn light had started penetrating the sky in the distance. The sun wasn't out, but it wasn't too far away. The streetlights had been switched off and the outlines of office buildings were visible in the fast depleting darkness. Another thirty minutes and the city would be busy with early birds – milkmen and newspaper-wallahs and joggers. This was far from ideal. We should have been out of Delhi by now. We hadn't called Udhham yet and he hadn't called us either, which was curious. He must really trust his confidants and their ability to deliver. Then I remembered that the office we had been working in had jammers installed to cut off mobile phone network coverage.

5.09 a.m. – 175 mm was the best part of an inch. It doesn't sound thick, but 175 mm of solid steel isn't easy to cut. We were on our sixth and final blade. Damodar gave the final push and the metal piece gave away and fell on the carpet.

I smiled and looked at Sylvia, and just that moment of distraction cost me.

'Hands up,' said Damodar, turning around. He hadn't extracted the painting. Instead, he had a Colt Python aimed at my head. He was five feet away and however unreliable a handgun might be, and however amateur a shooter he was, not too much could go wrong with your target that close.

'You shoot him, I shoot you, Damodar.' I only moved my eyes to see Sylvia, her right arm stretched out, aiming a handgun at Damodar. Her voice was firm. 'You shoot him, I shoot you. It's that simple, Mr Muscle, and I'm serious,' she repeated.

'What!' Damodar almost shrieked. 'Are you mad? We had a deal, remember? We are in this together, we agreed—'

'We agreed to nothing, Damodar. You spoke, I listened.'

'If something happens to me, Udhham Bhai will sell you like a cheap whore before he buries you alive, believe me.'

'Oh, really?'

'You cannot survive a day without my help. And you don't have the guts to shoot either. Is that gun even real?'

I stared at Damodar. He was talking to Sylvia, but he was looking straight at me, his arm stretched out, his finger on the trigger, his eyes steeling glances at Sylvia intermittently.

'Why don't you check that yourself, Damodar?' Sylvia taunted him, her voice like satin.

It was the three-second distraction I needed. Two things happened simultaneously – Damodar moved his upper body forty-five degrees right to readjust and refocus his arm on Sylvia instead of me. Sylvia had anticipated the move; she was prepared. She dived to her right and ducked under Bipin Patel's desk. I, seeing Damodar turn, rushed ahead on my left foot, and jammed the sole of my right as high as possible into Damodar's flank on the left. Damodar, though bigger than me, tripped, but he had already pulled the trigger and the bullet shot upwards and lodged somewhere high on the wall behind where Sylvia was a moment ago. The noise was deafening – the idiot hadn't attached the muffler. As he stumbled, his head hit the wall and the gun fell out of his hand. I had to make a split-second decision: rush for his gun or give him another hard kick in his groin while he was still off balance. I chose the latter. I hit his family jewels as hard as I possibly could. He groaned, cursed and went down like a tree trunk, and seemed out for the count.

'Fight's over, boyos.'

I turned around to see Sylvia back on her feet, holding a Glock aimed at us. A gleaming new Glock 17 – very familiar.

19

Friday night

Jattari, Uttar Pradesh

Night had fallen by the time Udhham Kumar reached Jattari. He went to see the work his boys had done and was pleased. The grave looked big enough for the Captain. One of the other reasons he had travelled all the way was to see the look on the Captain's face as he went down. Oh, it would be a delight to bury his wise-ass.

Udhham Kumar was all the more relaxed now. He had six men on the ground, plus Damodar coming along. Captain Vagh Pratap Singh had no chance. Moreover, the attack would be a total surprise.

Having driven non-stop for the day, Udhham Kumar had a couple of beers and slept for a few hours in the little tent his people had put up. According to his instructions, they brought him hot tea to wake him up around 1 a.m.

But the excitement started turning into disappointment, and then panic, when no call came. As per the plan, Sylvia was supposed to call him after they acquired the painting and before they started from Delhi. The call should have come in latest by 2.30 a.m. He didn't want to call since he wasn't aware of the circumstances there. If they had been caught, Udhham Kumar calling them at this unearthly hour would only make the police suspicious. He wasn't stupid to point them in his own direction.

Curiosity plus paranoia give you ulcers. And that was exactly what Udhham was experiencing at that very moment. The phone call, that assurance of acquisition, had already been delayed by three hours, if not more. What could have possibly gone wrong?

By 4.30 a.m., he could wait no more, and called Sylvia. However, he couldn't get through – a recorded message said Sylvia's number was not reachable.

He waited another half hour and then called Damodar, followed by a call to the Captain. Same result. How could it be that all their phones were out of range? And what had taken them so long to get into a vault? Wasn't the Captain known for his knack of breaking into any damn safe? The son-of-a-bitch was hardly proficient then. One more reason he should be buried.

Udhham Kumar had enough brains not to leave a message. He was furious, but there was little he could do besides wait. The thought that the three of them had schemed together and taken his painting elsewhere crossed his mind, but he knew it was his paranoia playing tricks on him. That would never happen.

He eventually heard the sound he had been waiting to hear all night at 6.23 a.m. His phone vibrated and buzzed. He pulled it out of his pocket and looked at the screen – Sylvia.

He received confirmation that the painting had been picked up. His team had done the job, even if they had taken longer than originally estimated. Damodar would call in the next ten minutes and then *Poppy Flowers* would be on its way to Udhham Kumar, finally.

The next concern hit him instantly. The entire operation had been planned keeping in mind the cover of darkness. How would they put up fake police barricades in broad daylight?

OVER A DECADE AGO

20

THE CAPTAIN'S STORY

The childhood setback I endured guaranteed that there was no place for me in the regular world, certainly not after I took to a life of crime. I never had a nine-to-five desk job, or any real job for that matter. I got contracts, big and small, to work for unscrupulous people and I got by on what I earned. But not every contract meant big money. I usually lived from job to job, and had no bank account or bank balance or hidden stash. The world I lived in didn't pay me enough to save or build assets. And I didn't shy away from spending on myself. I knew the hazards of the life I lived – I could be dead the next day or the next week. And I had no family or friends that I needed to leave an inheritance for.

But I learned to take care of my finances during the lean periods, when no one was looking for my talents. I found a simple job that took me only a few days from start to finish and brought in a cool thirty to fifty thousand rupees in cash.

I was deft at unlocking cars. Cars, even the luxury ones that supposedly came fitted with unbreakable locks, were a picnic for me. The Daewoo Cielo, the Mitsubishi Lancer, the Ford Escort, the Opel Astra – all were considered luxury cars at the time. It took me under five minutes to unlock and hotwire any of them. I had a partner who'd provide me with a truck and help me load the car into it and cover it with hay. I usually picked up the car at night and would cross the New Delhi border before midnight and arrive in Jaipur by dawn. I knew places where I could offload the car without questions and collect the cash. Depending on the make, model and condition of the car, I got a fraction of its market value, but even after expenses – fuel, truck hire, my friend's share – I still netted upwards of thirty grand most times.

It was on one of those trips to Jaipur that I took the spontaneous decision to stay back. I don't know why. But at the time, I had no idea that one single decision would change my life forever.

I strolled through Jaipur in the evening, savouring the famous lassi on Mirza Ismail Road, and enjoying the beautiful, flowering bougainvillea in soft purple and pink that added a more-than-generous icing to the Pink City. The sun was setting somewhere behind the buildings and the sky had a pink hue. A picture-perfect postcard tableau. I remembered how my father had wanted to move to Jaipur.

I checked into one of the five-star hotels on MI Road and gorged on some local dishes and ordered expensive Cognac. The crowd in the dining hall began to wane around 11 p.m. Most of the other guests were either families or friends or couples. No single ladies. I moved to the bar, and by 11.30 p.m., only the bartender and I were left. I guess he was waiting for me to leave. If I didn't go of my own volition, he'd have to wait for another half an hour, since the bar closed at midnight.

He came to me for the last order fifteen minutes before 12 a.m.

I asked for a refill of XO and we got talking.

In the course of our conversation, he gave me a number to call if I needed company.

'It's expensive, but exclusive,' he said with a randy smile.

'How expensive?'

'I wouldn't know. I've just been told it's expensive, sir.'

Expensive didn't bother me one bit. Even after the hotel stay and my evening out, I still had in excess of thirty thousand, hard cash in my pocket, as the vehicle I brought in today was in good nick. And an escort couldn't be that high-priced.

'And is she allowed in this hotel?'

'You'll have to go out to receive her when she calls and then escort her in … or I could bring her in, if you want.'

'How much to get her in?'

'Five-hundred rupees.' He didn't waste time deliberating; he had done this before.

'Is she any good?'

He nodded.

I called the number he had given me and spoke to a female voice, agreeing on seven thousand for whatever was left of the night. Then I gave the bartender his fee.

I'm not proud of everything I've done in the past, but no one is proud of their youthful indiscretions. I had previously picked up women at bars in Mumbai, but I had never called an escort to my hotel room. I convinced myself that it was the same thing; that only the modus operandi was different; that in those bars, too, I was paying for sex, which was disguised as company. And that night, I really, really wanted some company.

There was a slight knock on my door after a while. I looked at the clock: 12.43 a.m. The girl who walked in must have been in her early twenties; she was paralyzingly gorgeous. She must have been five-foot-seven, and wore a knee-length, black cocktail dress, like she was returning from a party, and open-toe stilettoes. She had a heart-shaped face, a sharp nose and a slightly pointed chin. Dimples appeared on her cheeks as she gave me an endearing smile. With subtle pink lipstick, black, shoulder-length hair – salon-dried and straightened – she gazed into my eyes, and I knew that nature could produce more colours than us humans could ever christen: she had double-shot-latte-with-a-dash-of-cream coloured eyes.

'You called for me, Mr Singh?' she asked, putting her leather clutch on the console next to the minibar.

'Yes,' I mumbled, my eyes not leaving her for a second.

'What can I do for you?'

'Do I pay you now or—'

'Are you in any kind of rush?'

'Not at all.'

'Then let's not talk about money.'

'I'm sorry, I didn't mean to—' I could feel my face reddening.

'Won't you offer me a drink?' she said.

'Of course. What will you have?'

'Whatever you are having.'

I had carried back the XO I had bought from the friendly bartender before the bar closed. I poured us some cognac and offered one of the crystal snifters to her.

'Thanks, and cheers.'

'What's your name?'

'Sylvia, but you can call me whatever you like.'

'Why would I call you anything else?'

'Some men do…'

'Well, I'm not like them, *Sylvia.*'

'And are you in one of the armed forces?'

'Nope.'

'Were you, ever?'

'No, why?'

'You look like a Captain in the army.'

'No such luck, I'm just a small-time businessman.'

'Can't be small time…' She took a sip, raised one of her eyebrows and let her eyes travel from one end of the room to the other emphasising, without words, that the luxury hotel I was staying in and the price of the room suggested otherwise.

'Oh, it's all on company expense.'

'And me? Am I some kind of a bonus too, a treat?'

I didn't know whether the answer should have been yes or no, so I just grinned like an idiot. And suddenly, a feeling of guilt took over. Wasn't I exploiting her need by using her body?

'You don't have to do this!' I had drunk too much, enough to be maudlin, and wanted to tell her she could take the money without offering her services.

'I don't have to do what, Captain? Are you saying you are sending me off after a glass of brandy?'

'Cognac.'

'Whatever. Am I supposed to go after I finish this drink? Is that it?'

'I mean, you don't have to leave right away…'

'Oh, I see. You want to be my hero. You bought me for the night, but unlike other men, won't exploit me but pay and send me away.'

'We could talk.' I was at a loss for words. I was sitting across from the most beautiful girl I had ever seen in my entire life, and I had paid her to sleep with me, and now I just wanted to sit and talk to her?

'Talk about what, Captain?'

'I told you, I'm not in the army.'

'Does it offend you if I call you Captain?'

'No.'

'So, what do you want to talk about, Captain?'

'Nothing in particular.'

'Captain, you are paying me seven thousand rupees and the night is fast turning to dawn. Some men would have made out with me once already in the time you've taken to serve me a drink. If you've changed your mind, I don't want your money. But could you be chivalrous enough to walk me down and put me in a cab, please?'

'No. You are not returning without the money I owe you.'

'Then I'll give you the service you called me for.' She stood up and looked around. 'Where's the bathroom?' She saw it before I could point it out and started walking towards it. She had a fabulous derrière. The muscle movement beneath her dress was no less than art.

She came out of the bathroom in five minutes. Dressed in black lace and silk lingerie.

'Like what you see, Captain?'

I nodded like a puppet.

'Wait till you see what's underneath. You want me to take them off or would you like to peel them off?'

'Sylvia,' I finally found my voice. 'Sit down, please.' I pointed to the chocolate leather sofa she had emptied before she had gone to undress.

She complied.

'Seriously, why are you an escort?'

'Oh my, my … not another one, please.' She looked up as if she was talking to someone above.

'I'm serious. Why do you do this?'

'Do you know how many men have asked me the same question and then forgotten all about it moments later?'

'I'm not like other men.'

'Do you know how many men have said *that* to me?'

'Try me.'

'Try you, how?'

'I promise I won't do anything you don't want me to do.'

'Captain, I'm not sure what your game is. I haven't come here to tell you my sob story. You've paid me to—'

'Paid you to?'

'You've paid me to fuck.'

'Nope. I agreed to pay you for your time. What I do in that time should be my choice, right?'

'Right. So, should I go back and wear my dress?' She gestured towards the bathroom with her eyes.

'No. I like seeing you without it.'

'Could I have another drink?'

'Why not?'

I refilled her snifter, but not mine; any more and I knew I'd talk even more nonsense.

'How old are you?'

'Thinking of adopting me?' She smiled wryly. 'Twenty-two.'

'And how long have you been doing this?'

'Doing what? Wearing this?' She ran a finger along her strap.

'You know what I mean,' I said, my voice thick.

'But I want you to ask me clearly, Captain.' She took a sip and raised her eyebrows over the rim of the glass. Mocking me, teasing me.

'How long have you been an escort?'

'Two years now. Wouldn't you want to know what my duties as an escort are?'

'We'll come to that later, if that's okay?'

Nod. Smirk.

'And you do this every night?'

'If I had been entertaining clients every day for the last two years minus my TOM, I'd have been a multimillionaire—'

'TOM? What does that mean?'

'You never heard of Urban Dictionary, Captain?'

'No. What is it?'

'It's the current generation's dictionary of slangs and phrases from around the world.'

'Oh. And what does *TOM* mean?'

'Time of Month.'

'So, this is a side business?'

'Nope. I'm a joy girl.'

'And what does a "joy girl" mean?' I had to admit, I was enjoying her company. She was as much of a talker as a looker.

'I love sex. I do it for the fun as much as for the money.'

'Why do you need—'

'Sex?' She laughed. She knew she was being impish.

'No … I mean the money.'

Sylvia told me her story from the beginning. Her father had had a sudden and fatal heart attack. Not that she came from an affluent family, but earlier, his monthly pay cheque used to take care of the household comfortably. But after his death, things had gotten harder, and now her mother was in the last stages of bone cancer. Palliative, but incurable, and the drugs cost a fortune. Sylvia worked in the hotel industry, but the salary couldn't pay for the medication and care. She was only in her first year of employment and the manager didn't see how she could be given any kind of an advance or a loan. The said manager had said he'd give her cash on the side if she was any good with blowjobs, which she had declined.

I felt sad as she narrated her past. What right did I have to make her dig up her wretched memories? But it did make me dwell upon how similar our histories had been. One minute, everything had been going for us, and the next minute, circumstances outside our control pushed us to change track. Every child should have a joyous childhood; unfortunately, ours carried comparable themes of aborted happiness. If she was selling her body, I wasn't a priest in some temple either. I was a conman; I also stole and had committed some pretty grave crimes for money. Nevertheless, both of us had one thing in common – we hadn't let circumstances break our spirit. We had taken up the challenge that those wretched events had thrown at us, and against all perceptible odds, we had striven to make our destinies. Yes, we had engaged in criminal activities. Yes, we had sinned. But we hadn't given up. We might not have shared it, but we had a kindred childhood.

'What about you, Captain?' Sylvia's voice interrupted my thoughts.

I told her some parts of my story, but kept the part about being a petty criminal hidden. Instead, I said that I ran a small-time motor spare parts business.

'We are like two peas in two different, yet similar, pods.' She passed a wry smile that betrayed the pain in her soul.

'Yes.' I recognised it was time to segue into something else. 'How's your mother now?'

'I could get a call any time, even tonight.'

'Like, now?'

'Sadly, yes.'

'So, what would happen if the call comes and you are with a…'

'You mean if a call comes and I've got a man on top of me?' She laughed drily. 'Captain, you are too much of a gentleman to be calling a hooker to your room. Are you a virgin? Have you ever been with a woman or will I have to teach you tonight?'

'You're not a hooker.' What was wrong with me that night? Was I too drunk? Or did I like her too much to accept, even to myself, that she was paid company?

There were minutes of silence. I got up and served her more cognac. Then we chatted more about inane things, taking care to avoid anything more about our pasts, or families, or sickness.

Soon, because I couldn't stay away, we made love and then lay there, a tangle of limbs, as the morning sun yawned and stretched and peeped through the curtains.

'Come with me?' I found myself whispering in her ear.

'Where to?'

'To Delhi.'

'Why? What will I do? And who will pay for my mother's care?'

'I will.'

'Are you still drunk?'

'I'm serious, Sylvia.'

She turned towards me. 'Who are you, Captain?'

'Why do you ask?'

'You didn't fuck me. We made love.'

'Is there a difference?'

'Trust me, I know.'

'Will you be my partner?' I asked without answering her question. Partner in what, I didn't know myself.

'I don't know anything about motors.'

I had forgotten I had lied about what I did.

'I'll teach you.'

'How much will you pay?' She said and bent over me to kiss me.

We chatted more. We made love again. We showered together. We called room service for breakfast.

Thirty-six hours after I had first seen Sylvia, I was in love. So I told her the truth. About everything.

I moved into Sylvia's small one-bedroom residence. She lived in a rundown, single bedroom studio in one of the back streets of Raja Park, which I was told was actually an upmarket area. I lived with her for a while. We were just two people in love, merely living in the moment. No one knew us. No one bothered us.

Sylvia's mother passed away three weeks after she and I first met in the hotel room.

We got married in Jaipur a month later. The terms and conditions of our marriage were simple. She would stop doing what she did and I promised I'd never bring up her past, under any circumstances, and would never let it come between us.

'But what will I do now?' she asked.

Sylvia wasn't a woman who could sit at home. She wanted to join me in doing what I did.

Well, till imprisonment do us part…!

We moved to Delhi. I stayed in a two-bedroom apartment in MayurVihar at the time.The rent wasn't low but it was nothing compared to central-Delhi prices. We had a few good years and a few equally fruitless ones. I mean, we didn't struggle to finance our meals, but it was just that. Rent, good food and comfortable living. We were aware that our little enterprise didn't have post-retirement benefits.

Nicking and transporting cars became a lot easier. I no longer needed a lorry to load them up. We merely changed the registration plates and drove out of Delhi in the middle of the night. No one suspected a couple driving on the highway. But with banks dispersing loans to spare part manufacturers, the fiscal realisation from stolen cars dropped. Either that or the supply had increased manifold. Maybe too many people thought it was a lucrative profession. Whatever the cause, the monetary benefit didn't justify the risks anymore. So, we got out of that business. Consequently, money started to dry up. We had been chasing our tails for quite a while, and I was racing towards forty. Though I still had a lot of good years left in me, those looking to hire me would soon start picking younger men. I refused to be a cheap resource just because some young rookie was cutting prices. And I didn't see my life as a street-side pickpocket either. We needed to up our game so that we could save. We needed to catch a big fish.

I taught Sylvia everything. Including how to fake documents, how to put on a disguise and how to penetrate a disguise. If there was one person who could see through my disguise, it was her. You see, you could change everything about yourself, your looks, your face, your body contours, your hairstyle and colour, your facial hair, the way you walk, the way you talk – just about everything. But a person cannot change their eye movements, its initial reflexes; the blink of the eye or the pure lack of it, the pupils, the reactions. They were a giveaway if you knew someone closely. And Sylvia was as close to me as anyone would ever be. I told her all my tricks because I knew she would never betray me. And if she did, I would be happy to take the fall. The way I saw it, if your best friend decided to desert you, you must have done something seriously wrong and you deserved what you got.

Sylvia was my friend. Not just any friend, my best friend. Sylvia was my wife. Well, we were *legally* divorced. I was under a lot of heat and I didn't want people going after her if they couldn't get to me. The divorce was a clever ploy for people to believe that we were no longer together and leave her alone. Anyway, marriages weren't prone to paper contracts. We both believed that marriage was a business of the heart. So was the divorce. The legal document could take a walk. I had never loved anyone like I loved Sylvia, and I knew I'd never be able to love anyone again. If she left me, I wouldn't have enough love left in me to share with anyone else. We loved each other from the day we met. And we would love each other till the day we die.

SATURDAY

21

THE CAPTAIN'S STORY

I looked back at Sylvia and blew her a kiss before Damodar groaned again.

'How could you—?'

'Damodar, you have a right to remain silent …' I mocked. 'Anything derogatory you say about Sylvia might be disastrous for you, under these circumstances.'

'What the fuck!' He tried getting up. He was a big guy and he was down simply because of a little distraction that had given me the first mover advantage. If we were both fit and standing, and neither of us had a weapon on us, he'd be a hard adversary to beat.

'I will shoot,' Sylvia warned him.

'No, you won't.' He didn't seem to be in any mood to take instructions from her or take her warnings seriously.

He was distracted again, and I punched him on the left side of his face as he turned. 'How about this?'

'Wait till I get my hands on you both,' he growled, his voice thick with pain.

'What makes you think you can?' I waved his Colt Python at him.

'Sylvia, don't listen to him, he's a rogue. You and I both work for bhai,' Damodar changed tactics.

'You do. I don't work for your bhai, I never worked for him.'

'What?'

'You heard it right, Damodar,' I said. 'Sylvia doesn't work for Udhham. And before you call me a rogue, you should reflect on what you were planning to do … swindle your own bhai, partner with Sylvia, kill me and make good with the painting, correct?'

He looked crestfallen. It was apparent that Sylvia hadn't kept his confidence.

'But why, Sylvia? What can he give you over the 50 per cent I had offered you?' he asked her and then, his brow suddenly cleared.

'Are you two an item?' he asked.

'Full marks to Damodar.' I laughed.

He looked at Sylvia, then at me.

'You should have told me that and we could have planned this entire thing together. Three's better than two,' Damodar said, backpedalling.

'No, it's not,' I said. 'If it's just the two of us, we keep the all the money; if we include you, it gets divided three-ways. Simple arithmetic goes against your logic of *three's-better-than-two*.'

'But I can help you,' he pressed.

'You've got five minutes to tell us how.' I looked at my watch. It was nearing 6 a.m. Some daylight had started permeating into Bipin Patel's office, despite the blinds being down. We had to get out of here.

'I can distract Udhham Kumar while you get away with the painting.' He elaborated a little on the *how*. It was a bit premature, as he hadn't had a chance to think it through, but if we all put our minds together and tweaked it a little, it could be a good subterfuge. 'And I only want five or ten crores, I don't care what you sell the painting for – I'm serious. I get my little share and I go back to my village to live with my mother and we never need to meet again.'

On the surface, it sounded like a good plan, but could we trust him? I prided myself on reading people. That was a key strength one needed to develop to survive in my profession. The teardrops in his eyes told me that he wasn't lying, but I also knew that this was because the walls had closed in on him.

'How can we trust you?' Sylvia said, her words mirroring my thoughts.

'You can shoot me now if you want. Because I know you won't leave me behind like this. If you tie me up, the police will catch me. And if and when Udhham Kumar or Bipin Patel find me, I'll die a painful death. But I'm not worried about myself. My worry is for my old mother. Before I die, I want to provide for her so she can spend her days comfortably,' he said in a voice choked with tears.

'Where is she?' I asked.

'I'll tell you everything, but do we have a deal?'

I couldn't explain why, or explain it in a rational manner but, in that moment, I trusted Damodar.

'What do you think?' I asked Sylvia.

She nodded. Still with her gun pointed at him, she allowed him to stand up. He came forward and shook my hand first, and then Sylvia's.

'Mumbai? I didn't think you were so naïve, Damodar. Bipin Patel might be an upright businessman here in Delhi, but in Mumbai he is a Matka King. His guys will hunt you down in less than twenty-four hours,' I told him when we were cocooned in a room in The Hind, planning our next move.

After retrieving the painting from the vault, we had exited the building without any unwarranted alarms. The watchman was nowhere in sight. He might have wandered off for his morning chores, but we were prepared. If he had been there and tried to stop us, it wouldn't have been good for him. However, him not being there meant that the unusual activity of three people leaving the building this early in the morning on a weekend might go unnoticed.

Despite our newfound partnership with Damodar, I stayed on my guard. A bit of extra caution never hurt anyone. Ideally, I wouldn't have wanted Sylvia to go into the hotel to book a room for us because she was exactly the kind of woman a receptionist would remember, but I also didn't want to leave her alone with Damodar. She booked us in and came back.

'We need to call Udhham now,' she said.

I looked at my watch. 6.23 a.m. Sylvia made the call and told him about how we had gotten delayed, and that we were leaving for Deoria shortly, taking the route he had outlined for us.

'Sorry we couldn't call earlier, Mr Kumar,' she said. 'We were in a soundproof room and there was no signal … it was an awfully strong safe … No, the Captain couldn't crack the lock. We had to saw it from four sides to gain access … oh yes, it is with me now.' She winked at us. 'We will be starting for Deoria in the next ten minutes … Of course, we'll take the

Aligarh Highway … okay, I'll make him call you as soon as he's back. He's gone to the loo.'

She was silent for a whole minute. Then, 'oh you're there already … would love to see you then … Bye.'

'Where is he already?' asked Damodar as soon as she'd disconnected the call.

'In Jattari. He's camped there, waiting for us.'

'What's he doing in Jattari? I thought the plan was that you two would dump me there and move on?' I said.

'He clearly doesn't trust any of us,' Damodar responded.

'The good part is that he won't be looking for us for the next ninety minutes or so. So, we must plan quickly and get out of here,' Sylvia reminded us. 'And, Damodar, he's asked you to call him after ten minutes.'

'Call after twenty. That gives us an additional ten minutes to think. Say you were stuck with me and didn't want to raise any suspicion by making a furtive call.'

Damodar nodded.

'We have two Glocks, a Colt and two Heckler & Koch sub-machine guns between us,' I told Damodar; Sylvia had known about them since the night I pinched them a year ago.

'You have it all planned, Captain.' Damodar appeared genuinely impressed.

Not everything. My mind was churning with possible places we could go to. Suddenly, an idea struck me.

'Where do you have to go, Damodar – where does your mother live?'

'Siddhartanagar, in Nepal.'

'You're from Nepal? What's your full name?'

'Damodar Yadav.'

'Okay, so let's go to Siddhartanagar,' I said. 'While we're in Indian Territory, Udhham, being a politician, would definitely ask for police help, albeit using his powers unofficially. Once we cross the border, he'll have less control. And once we are in Nepal, do you think you can use your connections to get Sylvia and me some documentation and passports?' I looked at Damodar.

'That should not be a problem,' he said. 'You'll have to stay there for three months, and we can always predate your records to six, and get you a domicile.'

'Great, thanks Damodar. That takes care of one big part of the problem,' I said.

Damodar smiled and then winced, pressing his palm to his left cheek. 'Shit. Why did you have to hit me so hard?'

'Well, it wasn't personal. If someone pulls a gun on you, I bet you'll do the same.'

Soon, it was time for Damodar to call Udhham. It was a pretty standard conversation. Udhham confirmed that we were taking the Delhi-Aligarh route, and that Sylvia was driving. He also told Damodar to give him a call again, when he was on how his, since there had been a slight change of plan. Udhham's goons couldn't put up a fake police barricade in broad daylight, but Udhham was planning something else, and he'd confirm when Damodar called in next.

Our ninety-minute clock had started.

We discussed our options of getting to Nepal. Flying was ruled out. None of us had passports and it would be impossible to get them – either genuine or forged – in the little time we had. In fact, we ruled out any form of public transport for the same reason. You need some kind of documentation to cross the border like that, whether it is by road or rail. Besides, with

Udhham Kumar's police contacts, he'd manage to intercept us easily on both bus stops and train stations.

'Does Udhham know you're from Siddhartanagar?' I asked Damodar.

'He knows I'm from Nepal. He doesn't know where from exactly.'

'So, when we go off the radar, it wouldn't exactly be hard for him to figure out that we might be heading towards the Nepal border … and we have all of UP to cross.' I was looking at various routes from Delhi to Nepal on Sylvia's screen.

We'd have to abandon the vehicles somewhere and do the last few kilometres on foot to escape border patrol. The India–Nepal border wasn't as well protected as the India–Pakistan border, and people still managed to get through. But the problem wasn't crossing the border into Nepal; the problem was reaching there.

Delhi–Agra Highway AH1 continued to Kanpur. We could hang left from there on to NH28 and drive up to Lucknow, and then Faizabad before forsaking it at Basti to take NH29, which would lead us to our destination. It was a little over 900 kilometres. But this was the fastest and the most convenient route and hence, Udhham would get it covered as soon as he figured out we had bolted.

Or we could keep driving on AH1, beyond Kanpur, get to Benares and take NH233, which would lead us directly to the same destination, and was similar in terms of distance in kilometres. However, with my past association with Benares known to Udhham Kumar, it was likely he'd send troops there to look for us.

And then it struck me that I was being stupid. The reason I was focussing on those routes was only because we had been asked by Udhham Kumar to take one route and we were looking at alternatives. But we didn't have to go there at all. There was a much shorter, less risky route, which, even with all possible detours, would be less than 400 kilometres, and in the worst of traffic, might take seven to eight hours, at the most.

'Why don't we head towards Bhimdatta? We take NH24/NH9 through Ghaziabad to Rampur, then NH87 towards Nainital and turn right from Rudrapur. From there, we'll look for the fastest route out of UP into Uttarakhand, and out of Udhham's realm?'

We decided that we wouldn't travel together. Whoever came after us would be looking for a trio. So instead, Damodar would drive alone, and Sylvia and I would travel together. The reason Sylvia and I had separated a year ago was because we had become very conspicuous together. Two of us were easier to spot, to remember. But now, I wasn't leaving Sylvia alone. Too dangerous.

The plan was to get to Bhajanpur – circa 350 kilometres – that was on NH125. We'd remain in touch with each other, but we needed to be cautious, as mobile location could be easily triangulated. Whoever got there first would wait for the other team at the old Hanuman Mandir that Damodar had told us about, and we'd cross the border together, either by paying someone off or figuring out another way, somehow. But if, for any reason, the team arriving late did not communicate and did not reach by the third day – Monday evening – the first would cross the border and wait another two days at Bhimdatta. If there was an inordinate delay, the first team would travel to Damodar's hometown and wait at his mother's house.

Damodar and I went down to the parking lot and retrieved our bags from my Audi's trunk – mine filled with all my goodies – guns, disguises, stripy decals to camouflage vehicles, and various magnetic registration plates.

We divided the contents. Damodar would carry his Colt and one H&K, and half the decals and number plates. Sylvia and I would carry the painting in our car. Damodar didn't protest.

'Brother,' he said, his eyes moist with tears, 'promise me one thing. Should something happen to me, you'll give my share to my mother.'

'You don't have to worry, but if something happens to us, I'm not sure how we'd get the painting to you.'

'Don't worry about that, nothing will happen to you two, but destroy the painting if you are cornered. I will go home and spend the rest of my life with the knowledge that at least we didn't let Udhham get the painting.' He winked.

Our ninety minutes were over. It was time to get going.

22

THE CAPTAIN'S STORY

Once Damodar left, Sylvia and I went to the room. She used the bathroom to change while I started working on my hair. We thought it was best to spend ten minutes to change our appearances before we started.

She came out wearing gold and green Ray-Ban aviators and they suited her perfectly. They were tucked into her new pageboy hairstyle. She wore figure hugging jeans and a short, white shirt, tight enough to show her toned biceps and flat abdomen. A thick, tan leather belt cinched her waist. My girl. I leaned in and kissed her – a long kiss. It had been longer than a while.

'Hello again, Captain,' she said as we pulled apart.

We kissed again. The second kiss felt even better. I had longed for that taste for a year. I had missed her every single day this last year. Our plan had been that, if nothing worked out during our separation, we'd get back together in a year or two anyway and leave town forever. She had consciously looked for a big job while I was in my self-imposed exile in

Benares. That's when she got scent of an old acquaintance, Udhham Kumar, looking for help. He had been passing feelers that a rather big job was in the offering for the right person. Some big larceny worth a figure with more zeroes than we could make sense of, she told me. She told me she had had a rendezvous with the guy once in the past, but that didn't bother me one iota. I trusted Sylvia. Her past was her past.

But neither of us wanted Sylvia to approach Udhham Kumar for the job. So instead, we orchestrated a chance meeting at the hotel in Lucknow. The rest was history.

My phone rang just as we were getting ready to leave – Sheena, my most ardent fan and student. I thought about not picking up the phone but then I did, and was I glad that I did.

'Hello, Albert, where have you been?'

'I am out of Delhi at the moment.'

'Where?'

'Mumbai.'

'Oh.'

'Anything urgent?'

'No, we were wondering if everything was okay. You didn't tell me that you were leaving the city.'

'Something came up all of a sudden.' I kept it vague. There was no need to elaborate or explain anything to her.

'When are you back?'

Never. 'Tuesday.'

'They told us you'd be back on Monday.'

'Sheena, could I call you back in an hour please?'

'Sure, I'll wait.'

I hung up and looked at Sylvia. 'She says she'll wait for my call. What do I tell her?'

But before Sylvia could reply, my phone rang. It was Sheena again. I was beginning to get worried. Something wasn't right.

'Hi, Sheena. What is it?'

'Oh, I forgot to tell you what I'd actually called for. I thought you'd want to know that Mr Bipin Patel's office was burgled last night and *Poppy Flowers* has been taken…'

'What! How do you know?'

'It's all over the news. The guard at the ATM in the building below heard a gunshot in the early hours. But the watchman wasn't at his post so he had to wait to report it, and by the time the man came back and went upstairs to check, the burglars were gone. But the safe had been broken into and the painting was missing.'

Shit!

'That's terrible. Sheena, I'm sorry. I'm with someone right now and I'll have to call you back.'

'But—'

I hung up.

23

Saturday morning

Jattari

Something wasn't kosher. Udhham Kumar sensed as much after he ended his call with Damodar. The other man hadn't sounded his normal self; it was best to put a trace on all the three mobile numbers to follow their travel.

Exactly one hour and thirty-five minutes after the call with Damodar, he received a call from his contacts tracing the phones. The three phones were still on and near the Connaught Circus area. He was livid. The first call he made was to Damodar, but he didn't pick up. He called the Captain next and his phone was engaged. Sylvia's phone rang but she didn't pick up either.

He was being taken for a royal ride. Those swindling bastards! They would die a sick street dog's death when he got them.

He ordered his contact to inform him as soon as either of the targets moved.

Then he called his people in Delhi.

New Delhi

Damodar didn't think he needed to change the registration plate of the Audi, since he was only going to use the car for ten or fifteen kilometres before jumping into another one. He didn't check his mobile or he'd have seen that there was already a missed call from Udhham Kumar. If he had, it could have been an early warning to switch off his mobile phone. In the rush that he was in, he started the car and gunned out of the parking. The sooner he got out of the hotel, the earlier he'd be able to change cars.

New Delhi

'What happened?' Sylvia asked when the Captain had hung up on Sheena.

'The theft has already been reported. We need to get out of this place as soon as possible.'

Sylvia pulled out her mobile.

'There is a missed call from Udhham,' she said.

'Switch off the phone, let's leave now.'

They got out and took the elevator down.

There was a silver Honda Civic in the hotel's parking lot. The Captain touched its bonnet. Cold. It meant it had been parked for a while. Maybe overnight. He pulled out a bunch of keys and opened it without any problem. Sylvia got into the passenger seat while the Captain went around to change the car's plates and put their bags in the boot. She secured the tube, carrying the painting under the driver's seat with a tape. He got in a moment later and started the car. As they drove out, she could hear a ruckus on their left. Traffic was already a mess with police arriving at Patel's office building in large numbers. Bipin Patel had clout indeed to be able to pull strings so quickly for a burglary.

'I'm sure Udhham Kumar will try and track us down. Call Damodar and tell him to switch off his phone immediately and turn off both our phones too, please,' the Captain said, as they turned left into Janpath, and floored the pedal.

She glanced at the Captain, who now looked like a seventy-year-old gentleman returning from a casino night with her, his arm candy. His wig – impossible to make out that it was a wig – was more white than black. He wore thick, black, tortoiseshell spectacles and had a handlebar moustache that could shame a real colonel. Even his facial skin matched his age – a well preserved, *Chyawanprash*-eating, healthy seventy-year-old. She wondered how he had managed all of it in merely ten minutes. Then again, it was a skill he had mastered over the last two decades.

Sylvia called Damodar and told him to switch off his phone, and only switch it on in case of an emergency, and that too, only briefly to text her. She'd pick up the messages when she switched on her own phone.

New Delhi

Irrespective of whoever applied their brains, regardless of which device they used – from an antediluvian abacus to the latest iPhone, two plus two would only provide anyone with one answer. Four. They could repeat the exercise as many times as they desired, but the outcome would not vary. Sub-inspector Hari Mohan Gupta had the smarts to unravel the mystery even in his half-awoken state. He usually woke up to a radio-alarm clock, tuned to the local news bulletin, and the local breaking news in Delhi that morning was the discovery of an art burglary. There was no mention of which art piece or the value, which he found odd, but his mind put two and two together without wasting a second. Art robbery and a conman in town masquerading as an art professor. It didn't need Einstein. So Udhham Kumar had hired Captain Vagh Pratap Singh for the burglary, which told him that the piece of stolen art had to be significant. He smiled at the irony. He had already identified the culprit before he even knew what had been stolen.

He got up, showered, dressed and made his way to Barakhamba Road.

New Delhi

Bipin Patel had called in all his chits. From members of parliament to the senior most police officers in the city, to the entire security staff of the building, everyone had had an early start. The police had cordoned off the area, and all other offices in the building had been closed for the day. The place was teeming with police and detectives. The crime scene experts were in full attendance, dusting for prints, searching for hairs and fibres, and adroitly digging to extract the bullet lodged in the concrete wall. The night watchman had been questioned and manhandled by Bipin Patel himself, before the cops had beaten up the poor man to see if he had any involvement in the burglary. When it was evident that he had been nothing more than negligent for abandoning his post, he was fired from his job. Every single person, from the cleaner to the janitor to the security personnel, was being retained and questioned.

Except for the vault and the bullet shot, Patel's sanctum sanctorum was intact, and after he had checked the contents of the safe, he was requested to move out of his office to let the police carry out its job without any interference.

Bipin Patel's vault had also stored a lot of cash and gold, but nothing except his previous *Poppy Flowers* had been filched. He was as outraged as he was flummoxed. Not many individuals were aware that he had the priceless painting in his collection, and even fewer knew that it had been locked up in his office.

'There is one Sub-Inspector Gupta here to see you, sir,' Patel's secretary called on the intercom. 'He says he might be able to help—'

'Tell him to speak to the DIG who's leading the team,' he growled.

'Sir, he says he knows who the burglar is.'

'Send him in.'

The door to his office opened and a bald, haggard man in plainclothes walked in.

'Is this a joke or an attempt to convince me to hire you as a private detective?'

'I can assure you it's neither. I have just one question, and your answer will tell me if I'm on the right track.'

'Shoot.'

'Do you know someone called Albert Rueben?'

Jattari

Udhham Kumar's phone chirped again.

'Where are they now?'

'They are not together any more, Udhham Bhai,' his source informed him.

'What do you mean?'

'Sylvia and the Captain are still near CP, while Damodar has left…'

Udhham had a moment of relief. Maybe there was some mix-up; maybe the other two had overpowered Damodar for a bit but he now had the painting and was driving to Jattari.

'But he hasn't taken the route you said he'd take,' the voice broke into his thoughts.

'What?'

'He should have carried on to the Noida Link Road, but instead, he turned left on NH24 towards Patparganj a couple of minutes ago.'

'So where is he now?'

'He switched off his phone a minute ago. We've lost him now.'

'Motherf—' Udhham Kumar couldn't control his rage any longer. 'Where are the other two?'

'They've switched off their phones too.'

Disconnecting the call, Udhham Kumar worked out his next move. If the theft had already been discovered, and if some camera had picked up either of the three burglars, Bipin Patel would get on their case. And the fools were still in Delhi, which was Patel's backyard. He'd get to them before Udhham could. It was best to offer assistance to Patel and hedge his bets. That way, they could share the booty. Sadly, the 200 million dollars would become a hundred, but it was either that or nothing. If they were still in Delhi, Bipin Patel had more firepower, and if they crossed over to UP, they would be at his mercy.

In the end, it was an easy decision.

New Delhi

Bipin Patel asked DIG Roshan Mehta, the police officer in-charge of the investigation, to join him and SI Gupta. Any doubts that either of the two had about SI Hari Mohan Gupta dissolved like Disprin in water when the old copper narrated the gist of his search for the conman Vagh Pratap Singh, aka the Captain. Patel's face reddened as he reflected on the visit from that phony professor with – who was it? – Sheena Marwah. Yes, and they had come to him with a reference from Jhunjhunwala. He wouldn't spare anyone. He took out his mobile phone and was going through his contacts to call Jhunjhunwala when it rang – *Unknown Caller.*

'Is that Mr Bipin Patel?' a male voice at the other end enquired.

'Who wants to know?'

'Mr Patel, it doesn't matter who I am, I know who took *Poppy Flowers* from your vault…'

'Well, I know who it was too.'

Then it struck Patel that the caller knew what had been stolen; he hadn't told anyone that yet, not even the police. He gestured to DIG Mehta and SI Gupta to keep silent as he listened to the caller talk.

Then he asked, 'So, who are you?'

'Again, that doesn't matter. I can help you get your painting back. I'll call you again in an hour. Be ready with your decision.'

'Who was it?' asked DIG Mehta when the call ended.

'Someone else knows who did this. He knows the name, same as what Inspector Gupta told me – Vagh Pratap Singh.'

'So my information was correct—' Hari Mohan said.

'Correct, but incomplete. The caller also had information on the Captain's accomplices. There were three people involved – two men and a woman.'

'How do you know that the caller is genuine? That his information is correct?'

'Because the guy also knows something I've told no one yet.'

'What's that?' asked the DIG.

'He knows what's been taken from the vault.'

'So what does the caller want?'

'He knows where the three thieves are headed. He says he has resources to catch them and bring them to me, provided I'm willing to give him 50 per cent of the value of the painting—'

'Which is?'

'100 million US dollars.'

'Fuckin' hell! What painting is it?' the DIG couldn't believe what he had heard.

'It's a rare nineteenth century antique.'

It had inadvertently erupted out his mouth, but he knew he now needed to cut the police out of loop as soon as he could. Maybe even Hari Mohan Gupta – why did he need him anymore?

New Delhi

Damodar drove into the Max Super Speciality Hospital parking in Patparganj. He exchanged the Audi for a slightly old, but well-maintained, Hyundai Accent that carried a doctor's red cross on its front and rear windshield. He put on the magnetic false registration plate and drove out, checking his watch. It had been a detour of just seven minutes.

But there was a big traffic hold up before Indirapuram. He patiently sat in the car, waiting at the same spot for almost twenty minutes. What was the problem? It was the Delhi border, he knew, but it wasn't usually so bad at this time of the day, and it was typically just the trucks that were held up. He switched off the ignition and got out, walking a few paces ahead to chat with the other drivers. It's a three-kilometre jam, someone told him. Apparently, there had been some problem in the capital and a thorough check on all vehicles was being conducted. The police had sealed all roads leading out of Delhi towards UP, Haryana and Rajasthan.

Fuck!

He had been told by Sylvia to keep his mobile phone off, but he had to relay a warning to them. He followed her instructions and switched on the mobile for two minutes to send a text. He saw no point in returning to his car. Even if the traffic moved, he would be stopped at a check-point, and who knew if they had his picture or description? Even if they didn't, there were other factors – he had no papers for the car, and the magnetic number plate he'd fitted would only fool someone from a distance. On close inspection, a policeman would easily spot it. And if that wasn't enough, he was carrying illegal firearms in a rucksack.

He knew he had to cross the border. And he knew he had to do it on foot. He picked up the rucksack from the car, locked it and walked into the densely populated area on his left.

Jattari

'Bhai, Damodar's phone was switched on, though only for a minute or so.'

Where has the bastard reached?'

'Around a kilometre or two before the UP border check post…'

A reptilian smile passed Udhham Kumar's lips. His source been right. He knew they'd be trying to get out of Delhi, and using his political contacts, he'd got a special squad dispatched. He could only get UP Police to cooperate with him, and the conniving bastards could still escape to Rajasthan or Haryana, and that had been his worry. But they hadn't. They were headed into UP. Why? Why would they want to come to UP, despite knowing that it was fraught with danger?

But where were the other two? Where were they headed? He couldn't believe that they'd move in a completely different direction. No, Udhham was sure that they would try and get to UP too. Perhaps they were using three different vehicles and had arranged to meet at some point.

The question was, where was that point?

'Bring me a map,' he shouted to one of his men. He'd figure out their destination and deploy his men accordingly.

He stared at the map. He needed to think like them. They wouldn't stay in UP, no. They knew that was his area. They needed a safe place. A place like home. One of their homes … Nepal.

Damodar was from Nepal. Suddenly, Udhham Kumar felt completely certain that they were headed towards the closest point on the India–Nepal border. He'd get them there. The bastards had underrated his intelligence. Class A idiots!

New Delhi

Bipin Patel wanted to do things his way now. He knew who had his painting. He also knew what his next step was going to be. He called up his contact in the Ministry and asked the DIG and his team to back off. It's not like they had recovered much from the crime scene – just the bullet and some fibres; there were no fingerprints at all. And with Patel not divulging what precisely was taken from his safe, there wasn't a lot the police could officially do.

Hari Mohan was dismissed from the scene too. A lone sheepdog couldn't hunt down three vicious wolves.

Bipin Patel had been through all the CCTV footage in the building three times. Now that he knew that the Captain was involved, it was easier to spot him on the screen, though the man's disguise had been excellent, and without Hari Mohan's revelation, he'd probably have gone unrecognised. The guy had also covered the cameras, probably to keep them from figuring out who his partners were… He hadn't expected the group who masterminded this burglary to be this dumb, or maybe they hadn't anticipated that their little caper would be detected within hours of their departure. There were people caught on camera leaving the building early on Saturday morning – two men and a woman – exactly like the caller had mentioned. What else did the caller know and more importantly, how had he known?

The more Bipin Patel thought about it, the more it seemed like there was only one reason for the caller to know this much about the robbery – he was part of it; involved somehow. Was he the man assisting the Captain in the heist, or was he a third person, involved but not present at the scene of crime? He couldn't think of a third scenario.

Well, he'd find out soon enough. He'd asked his sources to trace the call, and when the man called next, he'd have his number.

Soon, the phone rang.

'Mr Patel?' It was the same voice, but the background noise suggested the caller was outside, not in a room.

'Speaking, Mr…'

'For now, it doesn't matter who I am. So, what have you decided?'

'You mean, sharing the money with you if you catch the burglars whom we both know about now?'

'You don't know all three of them. And, believe me, even if you somehow pulled out their faces from the CCTV footage, that won't help you much. I have traces on their phones *and* I can tell you where they are at this moment. I could also tell you where they are headed.'

'Give me fifteen more minutes and I'll have an answer for you,' Bipin Patel said.

'It's your call, but remember, fifteen minutes could well mean that your painting is twenty kilometres further away from you,' the caller said, and hung up.

Within seconds, Bipin Patel's phone rang again. It was his source, with a number for the anonymous caller. The owner of the number was unlisted, but the call had come from a small town called Deoria, not far from Gorakhpur in UP. The current location, however, was triangulated as being near Jattari.

Bipin Patel hung up and dialled the new number.

'Udhham Kumar,' said a voice; the same voice that had been feeding him tidbits about the robbery.

'How's the weather in Jattari, Mr Udhham Kumar?'

'Oh, Bipin bhai, you didn't have to go through all the trouble, I would have told you who I was anyway…'

'It's no trouble. Let me tell you what else I think I know. I know you were somehow involved in the theft. I think your guys went rogue on you, and I know you are hunting for them as much as I am, right?'

You could say so …'

'And because you are concerned that you might not get the painting in your filthy hands, you want to partner with me now. You must be surprised I worked all this out.'

'Nope. On the contrary, I would have been surprised if a person of your means and intelligence hadn't figured all this out by now.'

'Here's my offer. It's my painting and I will give you nothing …'

'Your choice. Don't say I didn't warn you. If I get to them first, you'll neither get the painting nor a single paisa from me.'

'No, you didn't hear me out – I will give you nothing, and if I don't find my painting intact, you will pay for it. And you'll pay for it very dearly, Udhham.' Bipin Patel was raging now, his voice thundering down the line.

'You have no idea who you're talking to,' Udhham responded, equally angry.

'Oh, I know who I'm talking to, you fuckin' piece of shit.' Bipin Patel disconnected the call.

He called his head of security and instructed him to find the three people caught on camera. The video clips had been digitally cleaned and enhanced to reveal their faces.

His men were asked to prepare a file on Udhham Kumar too.

His men were asked to prepare a file on Udhham Kumar too.

Jattari

Udhham Kumar was both worried and relieved after his conversation with Bipin Patel. As far as he was concerned, he was untouchable in his own state. Patel could do jack shit once the painting got out of Delhi. And considering Damodar's direction of travel, he could be as close to certain as possible that the painting was travelling in the direction of Damodar's home turf. They would have avoided UP like a plague if the destination was anywhere else. It had to be Nepal.

He smiled. He'd have expected them to devise a smarter plan than that. Did the shitheads think that he wouldn't be able to chart their route?

He called off the search at the Delhi border and asked his police contacts to organise random police checks on NH24/

NH9. He also instructed the six men from his own team, currently in Jattari – bar the driver – to rush to NH9 and be stationed there, at least at two places.

Then he asked his driver to drive towards Hapur; NH9 was en-route.

New Delhi

Hari Mohan Gupta was disappointed, but he wasn't disheartened. He had no desire to help Bipin Patel. He figured that the painting Patel had been robbed of was one that he must have acquired by unscrupulous means – why else would he rather dismiss the police than disclose what had been taken? But the value of the painting had accidently slipped out of Patel's mouth, and that was enough to establish that this wasn't a petty crime.

However, Hari Mohan had no interest whatsoever in the painting or its value. His sole interest was in the Captain. Even on a weekend, it took him less than a minute to get in touch with the College of Art and procure the mobile number and residence address of the fraudulent professor, without giving away anything in return. He masked his number and called 'Professor Albert Ruebens' phone. No response. Then he called up an old contact and requested him to trace it. Soon, he was told that the number had been last used near Barakhamba Road around nine in the morning, which was odd. The time stamp of the three burglars fleeing the premises was around six in the morning. What were they doing so close to the scene of crime *three hours* after the heist?

He worked backwards, trying to make sense of things.

Professor Albert Rueben had come to Delhi for the painting – this much Hari Mohan was sure of. And as per his source, he also knew that Udhham Kumar was the last person to have met the fraudulent sanyasi before he came to Delhi. The Captain, he knew, did not have the wherewithal to indulge in a theft so big, and at a place whose owner was so nasty, unless the operation had been backed by some other heavyweight. Udhham Kumar was a dishonest, loaded politician. He fit the bill. The other two accomplices of the Captain had to be Udhham Kumar's confidants, sent along to keep the Captain in check. Thus, the random caller at Bipin Patel's office had to be Udhham Kumar, most likely calling because he wanted to partner with Patel to bring back the painting. And if that was the case, how had it all gone so wrong that two of his own aides had conspired to turn on him? Or had the Captain got rid of them already?

But why stick around for three hours? How had they stayed out of sight for that long? And then he saw the hotel opposite the building. Would they take such a risk? Check into a hotel just across the road from the scene of crime … hide almost in plain sight. Well, if anyone had the guts to do it, it was the Captain.

He reached the hotel and looked up the register, and the time stamp showed two men and one woman checking in early morning, just around the time the Captain and his team would have. Fake names, of course, but the receptionist described the woman with them perfectly. A strikingly beautiful woman, clearly.

While at the hotel, Hari Mohan also came to know that a car was reported stolen from the car park around the same time. A silver Honda Civic. Hari Mohan did not believe in coincidences.

24

THE CAPTAIN'S STORY

You'd have thought that to locate a million-dollar painting, and to break into Bipin Patel's office, *and* to literally saw a highly secured vault open, would put the most treacherous part of the operation behind us. But the going was getting tougher by the minute. Although I was used to hitches in plans, too many things were going wrong with this one. So much so that we were now seemingly trapped in Delhi, the last place on earth we should have been.

Sylvia had switched on her mobile for a second and we'd luckily seen Damodar's message – the police were apparently conducting random checks at the border without giving a reason. It could be my sheer paranoia, but I hazarded a calculated guess that the UP Police had started looking for us. With the robbery already reported, Delhi Police would be on to us too. And what's more, Bipin Patel and Udhham Kumar would have initiated the hunt too. It was scary and surreal – everyone and their dog would be hunting for us. Bearing in mind the life I'd lived, I had run into difficult situations a hundred times before but never into a hundred challenges simultaneously. You could beat or outrun one opponent, but this felt like an attack by various armies coming at us from every direction. It was a nightmare, whichever way I looked at it, and I was worried that it was only going to get worse.

But we'd come too far. We couldn't backtrack now and ask for a deal; we couldn't surrender or return the painting without any money in exchange and walk away. They'd only make us suffer before they killed us. Neither could we take them in a fight. We were two, and they were – well, I seriously didn't have the foggiest idea how many people were pursuing us. The pragmatic approach would have been to separate from Sylvia and somehow orchestrate things in a way that allowed her to slip away with the painting while I handled or distracted the hunters. I could always join her later. I tried convincing her of this, but she wouldn't listen to me. She argued that Damodar had already separated from us to do this very thing. In the end, we were left with just one outcome.

We were on the run.

At least, with the advance warning from Damodar, we decided that we needed to stop moving towards the UP border, at least till the police called off the checks. We decided to find some place in Delhi to rest and lie low for a few hours. We hadn't slept a wink the previous night and if this journey was going to take longer than we had planned, it was best to catch up on some sleep. Instead of turning left on to NH24, to go towards NH9, I continued straight on Mahatma Gandhi Marg so I could take a right that would take us towards Lajpat Nagar and a cheap hotel.

'Do you trust Damodar?' Sylvia asked as we entered Lajpat and I slowed the car down, looking for hotels that looked sufficiently dicey. We needed a place that wouldn't need ID cards and would accept cold cash.

Did I trust Damodar? I mean, only a few hours ago, the guy had me looking down the barrel of a gun, and I don't think he would have had any qualms about shooting me if Sylvia hadn't intervened. And now, he was warning us of the looming menace at the UP border.

'Do you?' I counter-questioned, glancing at her briefly.

'On one level, I do. He made it clear to me that he wanted to break away from Udhham – maybe it was some latent grudge, maybe it was pure last-minute greed – and he did stick to the plan. But on another level, if he can so easily forsake Udhham, for whom he has worked for years, why would he remain loyal to us?'

'You have valid points, but the one thing in his favour is that he let us take the painting. And without it, he's the one who loses. If he had feigned the coup against Udhham, where does that leave him now? Udhham will bury him in the grave he's dug for me if he goes back and tells his boss he's sorry he couldn't get the painting.'

'However, what if that too is part of the plan? He knows where we are headed, where we've arranged to meet, and that we have the painting. What if we risk our lives, smuggle the painting out of Delhi only to hand it over to him in the end? What if he grasses us out to Udhham and there's a reception party waiting for us to turn up?'

My stomach twisted at the suggestion that this entire race could end up with us in front of a firing squad. But I resisted.

'My gut tells me he's being honest. He wouldn't have given us his mother's address—'

'Which could very well be fake,' Sylvia said.

'When we stop, we can use a public telephone to call his mother. If she's for real, we trust him, and if he's lied to us, we cut him off. Agreed?'

'Yes.'

As we continued our hunt for a hotel, I stole a glance at Sylvia. The trouble with Sylvia was that you could disguise her as much as you wanted but if anyone looked for a woman as attractive as her, it would be nearly impossible to cloak her for long.

The only way to circumvent that was if they thought they weren't looking at a woman at all. It wasn't a bad idea.

'What's your bust size?' I abruptly asked.

'You shitting me, Captain?'

'Answer me, please. It's important.'

'What do you mean? Why is *that* important?'

'It's so I can figure out if we can bind your chest and make you look like a man.'

She cottoned on as I told her my plan.

'Well, we could definitely try, once we get to a hotel,' she said.

We found a relatively obscure, non-franchised, local hotel that looked like the ones people rent by the hour. Its signage was skewed to the left, with red lettering, that had once seen better days, faded to dull rust, and a recently whitewashed façade with paan-stains under the thin, fresh coat. All in all, it suited us. We parked at a distance, pulled out our bags and walked into the place. We were greeted by a welcoming infusion of odours – sweat, phenyl and floral incense sticks. The only man at the only counter looked at us like we were aliens. His eyes popped open when he saw Sylvia – she wasn't the type of clientele a hotel like this was used to.

'How may I help you?' he said to her, leering.

'We're looking for a double room,' I responded, and he reluctantly turned to face me.

'For how long?'

I looked up at the clock behind him. It was ten minutes to ten. 'A couple of hours, maybe three, tops.'

He looked at Sylvia, then at me. He drew the most obvious conclusion – an old man and a woman wanted to rent a room for a romp. I had no wish to set him right. It was better to let him think we were like hundreds of other people visiting his establishment. The art of staying anonymous was to never let anyone recollect anything specific or out of the ordinary about you, since people had a tendency to remember anecdotes.

'Okay, but you have to pay me in cash.'

'Sure.' No surprises there.

'It'll be 700 rupees.'

I handed him a 500-rupee note. He looked at it and pocketed it right away, without any effort at negotiation.

'Your good name?' He picked up a dirty register and a pen.

'Mrs and Mr Shastri.'

He knew I was lying. But I was sure he was accustomed to that too; most people who rented rooms in such a dump fibbed about a lot of things.

'Don't dirty the room much. The cleaner won't come until tomorrow now and I might need to rent it again.' He took out a set of keys from under his reception desk. 'Room 102, on the first floor,' he said, pointing towards the staircase.

'Anything on the ground floor?' I asked. Should there be a requirement, it would be easier to escape from.

'None.'

'Okay.'

'We should wait a few hours...' I said, entering and locking the hotel room behind me.

The aroma in the room wasn't vastly different from the hotel reception. Only the number of incense sticks burnt here might have been greater and ergo, the other two smells were masked better – but only slightly. There was a double bed in the room, a dressing table with a mirror, and a door that I presumed led to the bathroom. I walked to the only window and opened it. The place could do with some fresh air. There were no bars on the window, which was good. I looked down – eleven feet or so from the ground. Not ideal, but we could escape by jumping out of it, if necessary.

'Now, I think we should rest and figure out a way to get out of Delhi,' I said to Sylvia, dumping our bags in a corner.

'Aren't you forgetting something?' Sylvia said, walking over and wrapping her arms around me.

'What?' I said; my body responding to her touch immediately.

'I thought you wanted to check out my tits?' She pressed them firmly against me. 'It's been a year, Captain,' she murmured as I bent down to her upturned face. Our lips met and the smell of the room, the mess we were in, all of it faded instantly.

'I missed you,' I said as we pulled apart at last.

'Take me,' she responded.

I looked at the bed. The faded pink sheet looked washed but I wasn't so sure about the mattress underneath.

'On the floor,' Sylvia added.

'I have a better idea.'

Although the hotel looked dilapidated and shabby, the shower worked like a downpour. We made love standing under the cold shower; the rush of water overriding the sounds of our bodies moving together, our soft moans. I had almost forgotten what making love was like. But it was over too quickly.

And so we made love again.

'Switch on your phone and see if there's anything from Damodar,' I told Sylvia when we woke up after a couple of hours. I felt rested and clearheaded. 'I'll go out and make a call to his mother.' Using my own mobile wasn't wise, we had discussed. And in case somebody was tracing my calls, they'd get the Nepal number, too.

Damodar's mother turned out to be Damodar's mother.

Sylvia had received a text from Damodar only a few minutes back, telling us that he had already crossed the border and was taking a short break.

I switched on my mobile for a second. A voicemail from Sheena awaited me. Her voice trembled as she asked me if I had actually stolen Van Gogh's *Poppy Flowers* from Bipin Patel's office. She had gotten a call from him asking for an explanation, *'Albert, he says you are a conman, and if he finds you, he'll kill you. He's looking for you and the two other people who he says were with you…'*

So Bipin Patel had identified me as the burglar. And he also knew that there were three of us. That was quick.

25

'Lajpat Nagar? In *Delhi*?' Udhham Kumar almost yelled into the phone when he got to know that there had been short signal blips when Sylvia and then the Captain had switched on their respective mobile phones for a few seconds.

'And Damodar is somewhere near a town called Dasna, which is about ten kilometres from Ghaziabad.'

So the bastard had crossed into UP.

'I want the exact addresses for all of them,' Udhham Kumar said.

'Boss, that isn't possible unless—'

'Get them anyhow,' he said, and disconnected the call.

What the hell were Sylvia and the Captain still doing in Lajpat Nagar, he wondered. Why weren't they following Damodar into UP?

He looked at his map again. They were currently on NH235. If they stayed on this road, they'd intersect NH9 at the Hapur Bypass. He called one of the two groups of men he'd dispatched from Jattari and told them to travel to where he was headed, as quickly as possible, and wait for him there. The instruction for the other group was to go to Hapur, just in case Damodar got cute and decided to avoid the bypass.

Was it at all possible that Damodar had the painting, and that he had escaped Sylvia and the Captain and was headed into UP for protection? Was Udhham Kumar reading everything wrong? But then again, if Damodar hadn't been a turncoat, why hadn't he received a call confirming from him yet? Why was he keeping his mobile switched off?

Hari Mohan found the Captain's residence easily, and as he had expected, it was locked. He parked his Gypsy and walked around the house to check if any door or window was unlocked. No such luck. Thick curtains were drawn too, preventing him from getting even a glimpse of the interiors. He approached the neighbours, who had little to say about Professor Albert Rueben except that he was some kind of a recluse who kept to himself. He was polite, smiled and said hello if he ran into them and drove a black car, but that was as far as their information went. They did know the landlord of the Captain's house – a retired colonel who, fortunately, lived only five houses down.

Hari Mohan walked to the landlord's house and the man who opened the door was dressed and ready to go golfing, it seemed. He was in his late-fifties, with the trademark handlebar moustache and a beer-belly that strained the fitted t-shirt he wore.

'What can I do for you, Mr…'

'Senior Inspector Hari Mohan Gupta,' the Sub-inspector fibbed.

'Am I in any sort of trouble, Inspector Gupta?'

'Not at all. I just have a few questions about your tenant.'

'You mean Professor Rueben? Come on in. It won't take long as I hardly know anything about the man.' He chuckled.

He was candid. The house had been rented to Professor Rueben about ten months ago, but it had initially been seen, and taken possession of, by a very attractive lady called Sylvia, and his eyes shone as he mentioned her.

So Sylvia was the name of the woman accomplice, Hari Mohan thought as the colonel went on.

The rent was always paid on time, the money was transferred into his account from an account in Uttar Pradesh.

Udhham Kumar's account, Hari Mohan was sure. The pieces, just as Hari Mohan had expected, were falling into place.

The colonel had also spoken to some guy on the phone when he checked references for his tenant. It was a mobile number and the colonel still had it, although he hadn't called it ever again. It belonged to a Mr D. Yadav.

'His first name was Dhanpat or something, I can't remember,' the colonel said, apologetically.

The colonel had nothing further to add.

Hari Mohan walked back and sat in his vehicle. He wondered if the Yadav guy was Udhham Kumar's aide, a frontman; the politician might not have wanted to get involved in renting the property directly. Quite possible.

Or could Dhanpat – or whatever his name was – be the Captain's third partner? Maybe they had set it all up without Udhham Kumar's blessings? Or maybe they set it up with his blessings and kicked the mastermind's butt after the event? Hari Mohan was almost sure that he had the names of the trio who had taken the painting – the Captain, Sylvia and D. Yadav.

He put a trace on Yadav's mobile and seven minutes later, he received the info. That mobile was in a place called Dasna, off NH9.

So if he was right and these were the three people involved, they had left Delhi.

He called D. Yadav's number, but it went straight to voicemail. Hari Mohan left a short message – *I can help. Call me, I'm a friend.*

He was wondering if he should drive to Dasna when his phone rang. Professor Albert Reuben, aka the Captain, had switched on his mobile in the Lajpat Nagar area. Nothing made sense. Either he was wrong about Dhanpat or the three had split. One in Delhi. Another one on NH9. And where was Sylvia?

At least this gave him the impetus to drive to Lajpat Nagar. He couldn't comprehend why, almost seven hours after the heist, the Captain was still in Delhi. He knew the man was a sharp brain, but he was turning out to be a bit of a moron. Or was it that the Captain was waiting for someone? It couldn't be Udhham Kumar – that crooked politician was already selling him to Patel. Who then?

Maybe it was time to call Udhham Kumar.

Bipin Patel had called Sheena and raged at her, calling her that vile professor's whore, and accused her of being his partner in stealing the painting. He warned her that if he found out that she or her husband had played any part in the robbery, he'd strip her naked, get her raped by his men in the presence of her husband and then have her and her family killed.

The long and short of it was that it took him five minutes and twenty-one seconds to make her recite the Captain's residential address and mobile phone number. No, she didn't know where he was, and if he got in touch with her, she'd immediately report back to Mr Patel.

'You're not off the hook yet, you bitch. If I don't find him …' He grunted some other crude expletives and hung up.

By now, the car robbery in the hotel car park had been reported to Bipin Patel, and he'd discovered that the trio, after looting him, had camped in the hotel for hours after the robbery. His contact was also working to locate the Captain by tracing his mobile. Additionally, he had the manpower to hunt down the silver Honda Civic a lot faster.

26
THE CAPTAIN'S STORY

Sylvia sprayed a generous amount of tan on herself, to become two shades darker, and put on a baby pink, chiffon sari over a pair of jeans. We had tried and abandoned trying to make her look like a man. It just didn't work. In the event we had to escape on foot, she'd discard the sari. She had loosely thrown it over her head to make it look like she was going out for some ceremony.

I wore a sherwani over my jeans and t-shirt. It had got crumpled in my bag and the hotel did not have ironing facilities. I put on a baseball cap, pulled down low to cover my forehead, and put on large framed glasses to conceal most of my face. My previous make-up, of an elderly man, had washed off in the most pleasurable shower I had had in a year. The hotel manager wasn't at his desk, and we simply dropped off the keys and slipped out without any unnecessary chinwag.

It was time to abandon the Honda Civic. I pulled off its magnetic plates and left it where it was.

Meanwhile, Sylvia identified a white Tata Indigo across the street, a fairly common sight on Indian roads and far less conspicuous than a Honda. I pulled out a new set of plates from my bag and put them on, opened the car, started it and looked in the wing mirror before moving. There wasn't any traffic coming from behind in this residential area, but two Mahindra Scorpios raced by in the opposite direction and abruptly came to a halt about five hundred metres behind me, near the Honda Civic I had abandoned minutes ago. A man stepped out from the front passenger side even before the Scorpio had come to a complete halt. The man was none other than Bipin Patel. And then, a soft-top white Maruti Gypsy coming from the opposite direction caught my attention as its driver pressed hard on his brakes, stopping before it had crossed us. I saw him – a balding man, probably in his fifties – gawking at Bipin Patel and his men hovering around the Honda Civic. Now, who in the name of the dear devil was he? Whoever he was, he certainly knew Bipin Patel and by sheer inference, probably knew about the heist. But why would he follow Bipin Patel around? Or was he independently looking for us? And if he was, who else was independently coming after us?

'We need new phones,' I told Sylvia as I pulled out of there, our heads low and speed easy. Anyway, both the new entrants on the scene had their attention on the Honda. No one noticed our inconspicuous Indigo.

'Yes,' Sylvia said, nodding.

'Bipin Patel is already on to us. We were saved by a few auspicious seconds.' I gestured towards the mirror on her side.

I saw Sylvia bending forward in her seat to glance into the wing mirror.

'He knew about the car we took from the hotel and there is no other way Bipin Patel could have tracked us down to this place except through either of our mobile phones. Most probably mine, as he might have forced my number from Sheena or the college. And, Udhham Kumar has all our three numbers.' I had known that our pursuers would triangulate our locations through our mobile phones, but it unsettled me how quickly they had put it all together.

'Where do we get them from?' Sylvia asked about the new phones.

'We'll find a way, but first, we need to put some distance between them and us.' I picked up speed when we were far enough.

A kilometre down the road, I came up with an idea and told Sylvia that we should play a little cat and mouse game with our tails. Now that we knew how they were monitoring and stalking us, if my plan threw even one faction off our scent, it would mean one less set of predators we had to worry about. Hence, instead of taking the shortest route to our destination, I proposed that we take a detour. What was the worst that could happen – we were getting delayed anyway, right? We'd go to Indira Gandhi International Airport, switch on my mobile for a few minutes to let it feature on their radar, maybe change cars, and take the Noida-Greater Noida Expressway to make our way to NH9 through some interior route.

When we arrived at the airport, Sylvia came up with a terrific idea. 'Why don't we buy tickets for an evening flight somewhere?'

'You mean…?' I realised what she was proposing and my heart filled with pride. I had mentored Sylvia since we had met, and she had not only picked up what I imparted, but gone a step ahead. If something happened to me, I was confident Sylvia could more than look after herself.

'Precisely. Whoever takes the bait and comes to the airport would sniff around to see if we are flying out – I mean, why else would we have come to the airport, right? So why not feed them more scraps. And anyway, it's Udhham bhai's money we are shelling out.' She sneered.

'Brilliant idea,' I concurred.

We bought two tickets to Mumbai for the evening flight leaving shortly after 8.30 p.m. I hoped this would work, but we still needed to be careful.

One of the major concerns was that there had been an absolute lull from Udhham Kumar. Neither of us believed that he had given up the hunt for us, and the painting, and carried on with his life. He was surely out there, searching for us.

We were spoilt for choice in the airport parking – Mercedes, BMW, Jaguar – but we both knew those cars would be far too conspicuous on the interior roads in Uttar Pradesh and we might need to halt at hotels of the ilk that we had spent a few hours in at Lajpat Nagar. Imagine a gleaming Jaguar parked outside a rundown, sleazy hotel. No, our lot in life was to pick one of the few Mahindra SUVs there, and we picked a newish, silver one, a Xylo. It looked rugged enough for the terrain we'd be driving on. I had packed some decals and took an extra few minutes to stick navy blue stripes on its sides to give it an instant makeover; even its owner would fail to recognise it if we just drove by him without stopping, especially after I changed its registration plates. I switched on my mobile only when we were ready to go. On, two minutes by the watch and off: a shorter time might have indicated that we were playing them.

The air-conditioning in the Xylo was a million times better than the previous car. We enjoyed the cool blast for another minute before we were on our way, out of the airport: a couple, traditionally attired, going to attend some ceremony.

27

Bipin Patel only had the Captain's mobile number. He did not know the other two accomplices, and as such, he was oblivious that the team had split until late. His rogues had been competent enough to locate the car that was stolen from the hotel. It had taken them the best part of an hour to canvass around and find out where the Captain and the *girl* had been as Mrs and Mr Shastri. The hotel manager took half a second to confirm that the picture Patel's men showed had a striking resemblance to Mrs Shastri, though Mr Shastri looked a lot older than the man in the photograph. But Bipin Patel already knew that the Captain was a master of disguise; he'd fooled the authorities and experts in the past, he'd fooled Patel, too, as a professor. Hoodwinking the hotel manager would have been child's play. What cheered him, albeit momentarily, was that the girl – Mrs Shastri, his foot – was fairly recognisable even after makeup and wig. But where was the third conspirator? He could be anywhere, maybe he was the one carrying the painting and these two were merely bottom feeders trying to deflect his attention, buying time for the other guy to get farther.

Not good!

Bipin Patel wasn't dumb. Someone who ran an illegal empire – however vile, corrupt or disgusting – had to have enough brains to circumvent the law without getting fingers pointed at him. However, even the wisest of men made poor choices, especially when they had incomplete information. And hence, when the information came in that the Captain's phone had beeped at Indira Gandhi International Airport, it didn't require too much mental crunching. The Captain, with or without the girl, was planning to fly out of the city; worse still, out of the country. Bipin Patel and his men needed to get there before the bastard got on that plane.

Hari Mohan Gupta's information suggested that the Captain was at the airport. But he reacted differently. If the Captain and Sylvia were at the airport already, they might just take the next flight out to get out of Delhi. Was there any point in him racing to the airport? By the time he got there, they might already be gone. Instead, he turned and sped towards Dasna, trying to call Mr D. Yadav once again.

Udhham Kumar's face looked like the inside of a watermelon when he got the news that the Captain and Sylvia were at the airport. There was no way he could get there in reasonable time.

'I'll find them later. Let's keep moving and nab Damodar,' he told his driver. He was now certain that Damodar was in cahoots with the other two. Why else would one group leave everything for the other and just walk away after committing a multi-million-dollar robbery? Of course, the two scumbags were taking a flight to Nepal. If he caught Damodar, he'd peel the skin off his balls till the bastard led him to his two comrades and the painting.

'How far are we now?'

'Thirty-odd kilometres to go, Udhham bhai.'

Udhham called his other two teams to check how far they were from the agreed meeting point.

'Bhai, there is a petrol station on the left-hand corner where NH235 meets NH9. We are here, waiting.'

'Good.' He ended the call. 'Drive faster.'

On their arrival at the airport, Bipin Patel instructed his seven men to spread out and search for the Captain and the girl, and find out if they had bought tickets for a flight, and if so, whether it had taken off. If the three were together they'd be easy to spot, but they could have split temporarily to meet later in the aircraft. Or if they were smarter, they could possibly be taking different flights. He had already called in favours and the Airport Duty Manager, Mr Ram Narayan, was waiting for him.

'Sorry about the bother, Mr Narayan,' Patel said as he walked into the manager's office.

'It's a pleasure, Mr Patel. I have already tracked the man and woman you're looking for.'

'Really? Where?'

'Mr Vagh Pratap Singh and his wife, Mrs Sylvia Singh, are booked on the 8.50 p.m. Jet Airways flight to Mumbai.'

Sylvia. He knew the name of one of the Captain's accessories now.

'Thank you, Mr Narayan. What time will they be checking in?' Patel looked at his watch, trying to control his excitement. It was getting close to 5 p.m.

'They should check in at least thirty minutes before departure but they can check in earlier as well.'

To confirm they had the right people, on Patel's insistence, Narayan called in the booking girl from the Jet counter where the Captain and Sylvia had purchased their tickets for cash. She recognised Sylvia instantly, though she said the lady who bought the tickets was much darker than the one in the picture and she wore a sari, like she was going for a wedding or some formal function.

'Could you put a note at the check-in desk to inform you the moment they come in, please?'

'Of course, Mr Patel. I'll arrange for some snag in their check-in so that they have to see me before they can pass through. And I'll call you on your mobile before they get here.'

Bipin Patel thanked Narayan and walked out to call his guys. He wanted four of them to take positions near the check-in desk right away. The remaining men would keep scouting for any sighting of the pair in the airport.

Only three-and-half hours more and he'd at least have two out of three in his custody.

28

THE CAPTAIN'S STORY

We crossed the Noida-Greater Noida Expressway, and passed through Greater Noida taking purposeful turns in and out of streets, being careful to keep checking whether we were being followed. Nada. Someone once explained to me that there was an immense difference between 'seeing' and 'looking out'. In simple terms, *to see* was passive. You saw something, your mind processed it, drew some conclusion before it reacted and only then did you follow up with an action. More of a reaction. *To look out* was active. Your mind had already drawn a conclusion – in our case, the forgone conclusion was that we were being followed – and therefore, the plan to act was already in place; you looked for the slightest evidence to support it and took action if you sensed a hazard. There was a marked difference. And the difference here could be the difference between life and death. If we saw something at the last minute, it might already be too late. So we were watchful – to act, maybe speed up, maybe draw those Glocks out, maybe pull out the Heckler & Koch out of the bag that was on the rear seat.

We swung right towards Dadri and crossed it to take a side road instead of driving on the highway itself. The road was a bit bumpy and it killed a bit of the car's speed, but it was a much shorter route.

We had bought two new pay-as-you-go SIM cards from the airport but, unfortunately, we had to show our driving licences to procure them. So anyone scrutinising the time we spent at the airport with appropriate clout could easily find the new numbers, but it was all a question of timing. The more time they took in discovering it, the further away we'd be. We had decided to keep our phones switched off, and so there had been no communication with Damodar since the text Sylvia had received back at the hotel in Lajpat Nagar. We assumed he was racing towards the Indo–Nepal border too.

'Do you think they took the bait?' Sylvia asked.

'Can't say. Quite frankly, we don't know how many teams are chasing us. But even if your scheme has taken one team away from us, it'll be of great help. Once we get on to the NH9, we'd—*shit*!' I paused and took my foot off the accelerator.

'What happened?' Sylvia saw it a second later. A police barrier had been erected two kilometres down the road. Large oil drums were arranged across the road and five policemen peeped into the vehicles for cursory once-overs. If they were looking for a man and a gorgeous woman, they'd certainly stop us. No doubt about it. It could simply be a routine check or it could be specifically for us. There was no way of knowing. But it would be too risky to drive up to find out.

'What now?'

'We can't take a risk. If this has been instigated by Udhham Kumar, then they'd be looking for us, so we need to drive back a kilometre or two and rethink.'

We turned around.

There was little point in returning to Delhi. I drove slowly for a while until I had an idea that I thought could possibly work.

'We need to split up for a short while.'

Sylvia began shaking her head, but I put up a hand to stop her.

'Together, we are conspicuous. Alone and disguised, there is a lower chance of us being noticed. Especially if the police are looking for a couple,' I explained.

'But where do we find another car?'

'I've got a plan, my love.' I took a U-turn after three kilometres, drove a few hundred metres, and then pulled over. 'Let's get down.'

Sylvia narrowed her eyes but nodded.

I got down and pulled up the heavy bonnet of the car to make it look like it was broken. 'We wait until we find someone coming our way, then we request them to give you a lift; we say that our vehicle's broken down and as it is getting dark soon, it's best you go with them. I'll start ten minutes after you, and catch up with you after the check post.'

'What do we tell them about where we are going?'

'We are returning from a wedding in Greater Noida and are driving to Dehradun.'

'Hmm…'

'And take the bag with you.'

'Why?'

'It's less likely to be checked if it's with you, but keep it safe – it's got the painting and the H&K.'

'Yes, Captain.' She gave me a mock salute.

We exchanged our new mobile numbers, just in case something unexpected happened.

Five minutes later, a black Mahindra Xylo – same model as ours – came along. We could see an old couple, and it appeared to be slowing as it neared us.

The plan worked. I packed Sylvia into the vehicle with the bag. She looked like their daughter or daughter-in-law. No chance of the police smelling anything dubious.

I waved them off, waited ten minutes and fired the engine of my Xylo.

I slowed down as I approached the drum barriers and, like any other driver, smoothly snaked around them with my left hand on the steering. My right hand was wrapped around the Glock in the little door pocket of the jeep. Just in case. One of the policemen, among the six, carried a rifle. I had no intentions of shooting men in uniform, but if the policeman opened fire first...

And then, just like that, I was through.

I didn't burn the rubber immediately after leaving the spot and pushed the vehicle harder only after a kilometre. I reckoned the old couple Sylvia had gone with would be doing seventy, and I was moving at a 100 kmph. With a ten-minute head start over me, they had twelve kilometres on me if my assumption was correct. I saw the black Xylo in the distance about ten minutes after I left the police check post.

I flashed my lights when I got closer and the old man pulled over.

'It started after you all left,' I explained, without being asked. It's funny how guilt always spilled out. 'Something had blocked the fuel pipe…'

'They mix all sorts of things in diesel these days. Anyway, the good thing is you're back on the road.'

We thanked the couple, said our goodbyes and drove towards NH9.

29

Damodar woke up with a start and looked at the time. It had just gone past 6 p.m. He hadn't just overslept; he had passed out due to fatigue. He had reached Dasna, making most of his way on foot before picking up a car from a parking lot of a small market place. He had then checked into a sleazy looking hotel in Dasna and collapsed on the bed.

He now sat up and switched on his mobile phone. There were two text messages and eighteen missed calls from various numbers. Some numbers he could recognise – Udhham Kumar and his men – others he didn't. Sylvia had sent a short text asking him to buy a new SIM card and to contact her on a new number. The second text from an unknown number read: *'I can help. Call me, I'm a friend.'* There was no name. Who was it? Should he call back? What was the harm? He was getting a new phone anyway.

'Mr Yadav?' The caller said as soon as he picked up.

'Yes, this is Damodar Yadav. Who is this?'

'Listen carefully, Damodar Yadav. We know that you, Sylvia and the Captain were involved in the robbery at Barakhamba Road—'

'I don't know anyone called Sylvia or any Captain. You've got the wrong number.' Damodar ended the call and switched off his phone.

Hari Mohan was only twenty-five kilometres from Dasna when Damodar – that was his correct name – called him. He instantly recognised that Damodar was lying. If he had said anything else, Hari Mohan might have believed in the man's innocence, but Damodar had claimed that he did not know Sylvia or the Captain, when only hours ago, the retired colonel had told him that Damodar had been the Captain's reference. The fact that Damodar had declined knowing Sylvia and the Captain and cut the call so abruptly, was enough reason for Hari Mohan to press his foot harder on the accelerator.

His contact called him a second later to confirm that Damodar was still in Dasna.

Udhham Kumar was slurping piping-hot tea in the front terrace of the petrol station on Hapur Bypass. There had been no new information on the whereabouts of Damodar. He didn't harbour much hope of hearing anything about Sylvia or the Captain either. At least not for a while, if they had indeed taken a flight. The next he'd hear of them would be when they landed and switched on their phones. But Damodar was the key. Even if he didn't have the painting in his possession, he'd know the hiding spot of the other two shitheads.

His only concern was resolved when his contact called him with Damodar's position.

'The bastard is still in Dasna,' he told his stooges after he had disconnected the call.

'Should we go and get him, bhai?' one of the men asked.

'No, he has to pass this way. Let's wait.'

'What if he goes through Hapur and doesn't take the bypass?'

'I have a plan.' He called the other team that he had stationed in Hapur. 'Shyam, drive three kilometres west from Hapur on NH9 and lie in wait, be alert, but don't be noticeable,' he barked into the phone. 'If you see Damodar, call me immediately and then follow him.'

After hanging up, Udhham went back to noisily sipping his tea. His army of apes looked at him, bewildered and unsure of what their boss was planning.

'Hapur is three kilometres from where we are now, right?'

Nods.

'So, if Shyam sees Damodar three kilometres out of Hapur and follows him, and we drive to Hapur from here, we'd all be at the same place at approximately the same time, right?'

The men stopped just short of an applause.

'Now, two of you take a car and drive west on the bypass. Stop around three kilometres out, and keep vigil. Same logic – you see Damodar, call me, and follow him. I'll call Shyam and tell him to join us if Damodar takes the bypass. And don't you worry, I'll call you to come along to the party if that son-of-a-bitch goes into the city. Now, leave immediately and take your position. Be alert but discreet.'

He took the last sip of sweet tea and asked his driver to get another cup.

Damodar left his car parked near the hotel and walked to the local market. There was a time when only specialist retailers used to stock mobile phones and SIM cards, but since the mobile revolution swept across the globe and India became the second largest user of mobiles in the world, every other hole-in-the-wall shop could fulfil your cell phone needs. As per Sylvia's instruction, Damodar bought a new SIM card, and then just as a safety measure, decided to invest in a cheap phone too.

He called Sylvia's new number as soon as his new one began working.

'They tracked us down through our phones,' Sylvia told him when she picked up. 'So, good that you've changed your number now.'

'But does that mean they might know I'm here in Dasna?'

'When did you last switch on the old phone?'

'Twenty minutes ago, maybe.'

'Hang on a minute …' Sylvia put him on speaker and the Captain's voice came in.

'Hey, Damodar. Yes, they surely would have traced you. It would be best if you switch on the old phone and leave it in Dasna just before you get out. That would make them think you're still there,' the Captain advised.

'Will do. Listen, some guy called and left me a voicemail saying he could help, so I called him back, but …' Damodar repeated what the unknown caller had said.

'Did he say who he was?'

'Nope, I hung up on him.'

'Good. It was foolish to call back on the unknown number, Damodar. It was clearly bait. Please don't do it again.'

'Roger that, Captain.' Damodar was contrite.

Sylvia and the Captain were about twenty kilometres from Dasna now, but they agreed that there was no point in Damodar waiting for them. They checked that they had charging cables for their mobile phones in the cars and decided to keep their new phones on for the next few hours, as they moved towards the agreed destination. That way, they'd be able to stay in touch.

Damodar walked back to his car and looked around. The supposed hotel car park was a rough wasteland – an explosion of rubble, rubbish and weeds. There were two old Ambassadors, just car shells parked on bricks as the wheels had been removed. Both the automobiles were in the exact same state of despair – seats ripped off, windshields and windows gone, doors taken out. But that also meant that there were many secret pockets to hide something should one wish to – say, a mobile phone. He switched on his old phone and shoved it inside the remains of one of the cars. Then he got into his own vehicle and drove off.

Hari Mohan Gupta was on the phone, as his contact had called to relay the information that Damodar's phone had been turned on and was in the vicinity of Hari Mohan's phone, visible on the same locater.

'Damodar is in close proximity to you, sir … close enough that you should be able to see him.'

'I can't see anyone here; this looks like an unpaved place people staying in this dump of a hotel across it might use to park their cars, but I can see no vehicle parked at the moment…'

'Why don't you hang up and call him? Maybe you'll be able to hear it ringing?'

'I'll try that …' Hari Mohan said, and hung up.

The phone rang three metres away from where Hari Mohan's Gypsy was idling. He cut the engine, stepped out and walked towards the sound. It was coming from inside the torn seat of a rotting car. Hari Mohan put his hand in and pulled out the ringing phone.

That Damodar had played him rather well. So, they knew that they were being tracked through their phones. Precisely why they had been switching them on for only a couple of minutes at a time. But if they were playing games, they might have played one at the airport too. Maybe the Captain and Sylvia weren't taking a flight. They too might have abandoned their phones or merely turned them on to lead everyone astray. Nevertheless, if they had branched off as teams, they had to be in touch with each other somehow. They surely had other phones. With Damodar's phone now in hand, he scrolled through other numbers the instrument had been used for. Besides his own number, he found Sylvia and Udhham Kumar's on the list of recent calls. He called back to give those two numbers to his contact back in Delhi. Who knew what would come out of that?

He returned his car and drove to a nearby market. There was an idea brewing in his mind. If Damodar had had his old phone in Dasna, he must have bought the new one here too. He panned the market for the right shop, and one caught his eye. It was a small shop, one of those outfits with a small frontage with its own signage sponsored by some company whose products they stocked. In this case, the signage advertised mobile phones.

Ten minutes later, Hari Mohan Gupta's contact in Delhi had traced Damodar's new phone, travelling eastwards on

NH9. Disturbingly, the contact also found Udhham Kumar twenty-odd kilometres away on the Hapur Bypass on NH9. If Udhham got to Damodar first…

Damodar hadn't yet stored the numbers by names in the new phone book and hence, accidentally picked up the incoming call when his phone rang.

'Damodar Yadav?'

'Who's this?'

'I called you before too, but it doesn't matter who I am; what matters is that I'm still coming after you. Worse, your friends are waiting for you at the Hapur Bypass…'

Damodar, recognising the voice from the previous call and realising his folly, cut the call, scrolled down and memorised Sylvia's new number and turned off the phone with lightning speed. *Friends at Hapur bypass?* What did the man mean? Had Sylvia and the Captain already arrived there? And how would this guy know about that anyway?

But with his new phone compromised, his plans had to change. He swerved the car off NH9 and right onto the Upper Ganga Canal Road. He drove fast and stopped after a few kilometres at a tiny roadside vendor. He ordered tea and handed the guy a 500 rupee note. 'Do you have a phone, my battery's dead.'

'Yes, sirji,' the man said, pocketing the note and pulling out his phone.

Damodar left his car and walked a furlong away from the stall to call Sylvia. He updated her about everything and asked, 'How come you guys have already reached Hapur Bypass? You must surely have overtaken me—'

'What are you talking about, Damodar? We are on NH9, just passed a sign on the right, showing a diversion to Dasna, but obviously we are continuing straight on the highway.'

'Chief, where are you?' The Captain's voice came on, urgent.

Damodar gave them his location.

'Did you say the guy who called you mentioned that he was behind you?' the Captain asked.

'Yes, but he could be bullshitting me, you know…'

'Okay, just wait there. We'll travel ahead from where you turned right and scope out what's going on, then turn around and come to you. Don't move until you hear from us. We'll call back on this number you're calling from.'

'Okay. Keep me informed.'

'And do not switch on your new phone under any circumstances,' the Captain said before hanging up.

'Are you seeing what I'm seeing?' the Captain asked, slowing down and gesturing towards a vehicle almost a kilometre ahead of them.

'A Maruti Gypsy,' responded Sylvia, raising her eyebrows in question.

'And where else did we see that white Gypsy?'

'You mean … shit!' She dug into her bag and pulled out a small pair of binoculars.

'I bet it has a DL4 registration plate and a middle-aged, bald man at the wheel.'

'Yes for DL4, yes for egg-shaped head, but determining his age from this distance is a bit difficult.'

'You want me to overtake him so we can see?' he quipped. These days, it was too much of a coincidence in itself to find two white Gypsys in a day – the model's heyday was long over. And to find both of them with a DL4 plate – West Delhi – and both being driven by a bald man, it had to be more than a coincidence. It had to be the same guy. They agreed that it had to be Udhham's or Bipin Patel's man, pretending to be friendly with Damodar to trap them.

'Before you switched off your old number, did you see if you had any missed calls from a mobile number that wasn't in your phonebook?'

'There were a few, but I assumed they were from Udhham, using someone else's phone. How about you?'

'Same.' The Captain pursed his lips.

'Damodar has his number…'

'We can't let Damodar switch his phone on. He'll get traced again…'

'What do you suggest we do?'

'Let me think.'

The signs for Hapur and Hapur Bypass had started to appear. In five kilometres, they had to make their decision about which way to turn.

'Who do you think are the friends the caller mentioned?' Sylvia asked. For the first time since the morning, she could feel real fear creeping in.

'Well, it can't be the caller's allies, or he wouldn't have warned Damodar. So either it's someone he didn't want getting to Damodar first … or there is no one at the bypass and this was just the caller's way of sending Damodar into Hapur city instead of the bypass. Maybe his men are waiting in there.'

'What do we do now?'

'We follow him. But before that, we'll stop for a second. You get into the rear cabin, take the rifle out and stay low and out of sight. I'll drive closer to see what's happening. We size up the opposition and then speak to Damodar.'

He pulled over and Sylvia jumped out and climbed right back into the rear seat. He waited for two cars to pass them and then drove off.

Udhham Kumar wasn't one to be short of cash or contacts. He had called a local Hapur zamindar and asked for a few musclemen to be sent to the petrol station where he was currently camped. The zamindar, misunderstanding the purpose, sent four men on a tractor. All able-bodied men who toiled the land, twelve to fourteen hours a day, but didn't have a criminal background and couldn't be counted as the sharpest tools, even in an antique toolbox. But they still counted as more bodies on the ground.

Udhham was highly strung at the moment. Losing the painting was only one part of the problem. If those three bastards escaped, his reputation would take a severe hit too. What would his men think? The people who worked for him needed to be scared of him, intimidated by his power. He had to make an example of them; such dissidence couldn't be forgiven.

He received information that Damodar's phone had continuously been on for the last three-quarters of an hour now, and that he was on the move, driving east on NH9, about five miles away from the junction where the road split between Hapur and Hapur Bypass. He called the men he had positioned on the outskirts of the city to be alert.

'What can you see now?' he asked.

'A white Gypsy, a Hyundai hatchback, a Maruti Swift and a Mahindra Xylo, but Damodar isn't in any of them, bhai.'

'Okay. Call me the minute you see that conniving bastard.'

30

THE CAPTAIN'S STORY

I saw it first – a silver Hyundai Accent a kilometre down the road on the left, parked at an angle on the uneven pavement next to the tarmac, facing our direction of travel and ahead of the vast untended wild trees and bushes. They could have hidden behind the vegetation and no one would have seen them, but it might have been difficult if they needed to chase down a vehicle. The driver sat in position, looking at passing vehicles and on the other side, a man stood looking into passing vehicles through powerful binoculars; a distance spotter and a close quarter one, surely waiting for someone. Bloody amateurs.

'Sylvia, are those people anyone you—'

'Udhham's men. I've seen them before.'

'Make sure you are completely hidden from view when we pass them.'

Ahead of us, the Gypsy passed the waiting men. There were two cars between him and us, and I couldn't see if he made any gestures or waved to communicate anything about us following. As far as I could see, he hadn't spotted us tailing him yet, but there was no way of knowing. The first car after the Gypsy was passing the point now. No reaction from the men in the parked car, although the couple in the car turned to see them. Same with the second car. Same for us. They didn't flinch or react when we drove by them. Obviously, they hadn't recognised me. The Gypsy in front was still maintaining its speed, but I raised my leg from the accelerator and let the car slow down.

'Can I sit up now?' Sylvia asked.

'Yes, we're safe.'

'What's wrong then … why are you slowing down?'

'Two reasons – one, we don't know what lies ahead and, two we need to take care of these guys first.'

'What are you going to do? Turn around and shoot them when we pass them this time?'

'No. I'll take this jeep off the road and park behind these trees.' I pointed at the overgrown, almost forest-like foliage on the side of the road. 'You take the wheel and sit tight. I'll walk back to where they are stationed and ask them a few questions. Then I'll call you, and we drive back to Damodar.'

Sylvia looked worried. 'It looked like there might be more than one man there. I don't want you to go alone. Let me come with you.'

'No, you stay here. I took a good look. It's just two men, and I'll take care of them.'

I took out a pair of handcuffs from the bag and walked back, moving slowly behind the trees. I didn't want to run and be out of breath by the time I faced my adversaries. Moreover,

I had to tread softly because I didn't know what weapons they had. The average man walks at the speed of 5 kmph, but I considered myself fitter than average, and I got there in eight minutes and some change. I could see them in the same position I had witnessed when I had passed in the car, which was great. They were in the best positions for me to approach from behind. The one standing and staring into binoculars had his back towards me and he successfully blocked the driver's sight if he looked my way. I walked in complete silence. I had to ensure they didn't see me or hear me till I was within one metre distance of the guy with binoculars. Luckily, I had been in situations before where I'd had to be in suspended animation and I had learnt to control and lower my breathing so that even a person next to me couldn't hear me inhale or exhale. Quite frankly, a surprise attack often worked better than an open one.

Thankfully, it was getting dark when I got there, and the traffic had almost ceased.

'Hello, I am guessing you are one of Udhham's monkeys,' I said coolly, after I had placed my Glock in the small of my adversary's back. 'I'm very sorry to rain on your parade, my friend.'

'Who the—'

'What you have against your back is a Glock, not my hard-on, and it wouldn't take me more than a second to pull the trigger. Best case, it will kill you; worst, it will damage your spine and put you in a wheelchair for life. I don't think you want either, do you?'

'Shyam,' he called aloud.

'What is it, Keshav?' I heard the driver's door open and slam shut and Shyam walked over to us. This guy was humungous.

He must have been around six-foot seven, and buffed. He could tear me from limb to limb one-handed.

'It's me, Shyam,' I waved at him with my left hand from behind Keshav, my right hand still holding the gun in place. 'And please don't come close; if I get too scared, my finger might twitch, and Keshav here might unnecessarily die.'

He stopped. 'Who the hell are you?'

It was obvious they hadn't recognised me. Should I pretend to be a psycho or should I let them know? 'I'm the Captain your boss has sent you looking for, but please don't bother to call him,' I said, as I saw him pulling a mobile out of his shirt's front pocket. 'Throw the phone here.' I pointed towards my feet. He glared at me for a moment, but then threw it softly.

'You won't get away from us.'

'Oh, but I will. Just wait and watch. Now Keshav ji, where is your phone?' I moved my left hand around and pulled his instrument out of his pocket before he could respond. 'Any more communication devices in the car?'

'No.'

'Are you sure? If I search and find any, it might cost me a bullet…'

'We don't have any more phones,' Shyam repeated.

'Any guns?'

'No.'

'Shyam, I want you to walk around the other side of the car, take a circle and come to my right near the rear wheel so I can see you. And please don't get cute with me, okay?'

He didn't respond, which was frankly very rude, but at least he took my order seriously and started moving immediately. And that was one of the biggest mistakes of my life. To underestimate the opposition, to think that your rivals were rookies, was in itself one of the biggest rookie mistakes. I hadn't wanted King Kong to pass behind my back or anywhere close to me while I held the gun to his comrade's back. What I totally missed was that if he walked from the other side, part of him would stay hidden behind the car while he circled it to reappear near the rear wheel on our side. That provided him with a few crucial seconds to pull out a gun. And as he returned to sight, he had a gun in his right hand, aimed at my head, since Keshav shielded the rest of my body.

'Your game is over, drop the gun or I'll shoot you.'

'You won't, I know.'

'Oh really?'

'I dare you.' But once again, I had grossly miscalculated. I saw Shyam's thick, sausage-sized finger jerk. He was indeed pressing the trigger. I had just about enough time to jump to my right, leaving Keshav standing, and witnessed the bullet hitting Keshav's forehead. I had been a small-time criminal for all my adult life, and seen bullets fired in films. But I had never seen a man get shot before. It was gross. I saw the bullet split open Keshav's head and blood, grey matter and whatnot, splatter in all directions. I turned and shot three bullets in Shyam's direction. I was mid-air when I shot, so I couldn't take aim, but given that he was disadvantageously built like a tank, I was certain at least one would hit him. And it appeared that one of them did. It hit his right thigh on the inside and a fountain of blood oozed out. He fell to the right, his body hitting the car and ricocheting in the opposite direction, the gun flying ten metres away from his hand, if not more. As he fell, I noticed that another bullet I had fired had hit him too, somewhere under his eye. He slumped and was still.

Shit!

I had come here to scare these guys into giving me info on Udhham. Instead, I had two bodies before me.

I called Sylvia, and till she got here, decided to rummage through their belongings. I started looking for their guns and mobiles. I pocketed the guns – both guys had been carrying Chinese QSWs semi-automatics; not the best pistols in the world, but considering the demo I'd just seen, clearly in working condition – and smashed their Samsung phones till there was no chance of any signal tracing them. I also bent down and let the air out of two of the tyres before I heard a vehicle approaching. It was Sylvia.

'What happened?' She got off and saw the bodies, and her face turned pale.

I gave her a quick recap. 'This is a mess, but we need to leave, now. Before anyone gets here and finds out what has happened. Let's get to Damodar. You drive,' I said to her and we got into the car.

'Are you alright?' Sylvia asked me.

'Yes, I guess, maybe still in a bit of shock.'

I spoke to Damodar and he gave us directions to the teashop. I told him we'd be there in half-an-hour or thereabouts. I decided it was best I didn't tell him about the deaths of his ex-colleagues.

We travelled in silence. It was pitch dark now and I looked at Sylvia as she drove. The lights from the instrument cluster of the vehicle dimly bounced off her face, making her look even more beautiful and unearthly. Maybe this was Meatloaf's *Paradise by the Dashboard Light,* after all.

31

Hari Mohan Gupta drove straight and turned right to get to the Hapur Bypass, where he knew Udhham Kumar was. It was best to join forces with Udhham to know more about the three fugitives. As he drove into the petrol station, he saw Udhham and his men rushing towards his Gypsy and then stopping.

'Mr Kumar?' he asked politely as he got out.

'Yes, who are you?'

'Delhi Police.' He showed his ID card.

'And where's Damodar?'

'Why would he be with me? I'm here to arrest Damodar and his two buddies.'

'How do you have Damodar's phone?'

That explained why they'd rushed towards him like that. He was carrying Damodar's discarded mobile phone that Udhham must have been tracking. He explained how Damodar had tricked him too.

'But I have his new number, I called him. He cut my call and switched off his phone. The last I know, he was travelling east on NH9, but he's disappeared since.'

'He didn't pass this way.' Udhham Kumar was bristling with anger.

'But he could have passed through the city—'

'He couldn't have, my men are stationed there and they'd have informed me if they saw him.'

'I know that, I saw them. But the question is, where did Damodar go?'

'No idea. Do you know the whereabouts of that Captain and that bitch?'

'When I checked last, they were at Delhi Airport, but considering Damodar bought a new phone to mislead us, maybe they did the same with theirs. So, for all we know, they could be coming this way as well…'

'But how can Damodar just disappear from the highway?'

'Let's put our heads together and think, Mr Kumar.'

With the check-in time having come and gone, and the flight having taken off, it was evident that Mrs Sylvia Singh and Mr Vagh Pratap Singh had given Bipin Patel a royal slip. Rage consumed him. His biggest regret was that too much time had elapsed since they had been at the airport, waiting, and that had given the thieves ample time to go wherever they wanted.

Maybe it was time to call Udhham Kumar after all.

When there was no response to his repeated calls, Udhham sent one of his other men to take a quick round to check on

Shyam and Keshav. He couldn't believe it when he heard that they were dead. Shot.

Sub-inspector Gupta joined him and they travelled together to the scene of the crime. The tableau suggested that they hadn't been shot from a passing vehicle. Someone had been there on foot. Udhham let the policeman do his job, and he was clear about the fact that nothing should come back to him; that he wouldn't even acknowledge knowing them if someone asked him.

But he was furious. How could they have been so negligent to let themselves get killed? How had someone just sneaked up on them like that? Were they flipping deaf as well as blind? Or drunk?

He stationed two other men at a new post on the road that lead into the city and moved back to the camp he had set up at the petrol station on the bypass. Along the way, he called up everyone that he knew to request for more manpower. By 10 p.m., several roadblocks and setups were in place within a 200 km diameter of Hapur. According to SI Gupta, the dead men had been alive when he had passed them on his way to Udhham. That gave the assailants a two-hour window and the best they could have done was 150-200 km in direction. Udhham had promised rewards for information on, or capture of, any of the three people on the run.

SI Gupta told Udhham about the conversation he'd had with Damodar, and how he had told the man about Udhham Kumar's men waiting for him at the bypass.

'So if they know you are here, they'd be least likely to take this route,' Udhham said.

'Wrong. This is the most likely route they'd take, I think,' the sub-inspector said.

'What do you mean?'

'It's pure logic. They'd assume you'd think this, that there's no way they are coming here if they know it's where you are waiting.'

'I see what you mean.'

'So let's wait here. I'll stay with you for a while until I decide what to do next,' SI Gupta said.

Beers were bought from a nearby village store and served.

'What brings you here, inspector sahib?'

'It's a long story.'

'Let's hear it.'

'To be honest with you,' started Hari Mohan, sipping the beer from a steel tumbler, 'I don't even know what was stolen from Mr Bipin Patel's locker. I mean, I know it is something valuable, a piece of art, but I have no idea what it is and honestly, I have no interest in that part of things. All I want is to bring Vagh Pratap Singh, aka the Captain, to justice—'

'So you don't know that the painting is the precious *Poppy Flowers* by Vincent van Gogh?'

'Not until now, but how did a Van Gogh painting come into Bipin Patel's possession in the first place?

'Oh, that is an even longer story than yours...'

'Let's hear it then.'

'What happened to your threats?' Udhham Kumar taunted.

'I was misled –' Bipin Patel said through gritted teeth. He could tell that the son-of-a-bitch was enjoying himself.

'To the Delhi airport?' Udhham's snigger was perceptible over the phone.

'Listen, Mr Kumar...' Bipin Patel swallowed whatever pride he had left, discerning that it was time to put away his trumpet rather than blow it. The three scoundrels had escaped with the painting and were out of his reach. The probability of the painting's retrieval was now low, if not zero, and he needed to make peace with the crooked politician if he was to have a chance at all. 'I'm really sorry, but I'm sure you can appreciate I was under stress, and I made the mistake of not recognising that you were a friend who was only trying to help...'

'fifty-five, forty-five,' Udhham interrupted him.

'What?'

'The offer is now 55 per cent in my favour. You get 45 per cent if I capture them and get the painting.'

'Agreed,' the other man said eagerly. He was clutching at straws. 'But will you handover those guys to me, please?'

'Not the girl; the girl is mine. And I need you to deploy your men, really good men, where I tell you to. Is that okay?'

'Of course, Mr Kumar. But do you know where they are?' Bipin Patel asked, keeping his tone conciliatory.

'Yes. I'll call you in two hours and let you know.'

'Thank you.'

'Flippin turd,' Bipin Patel yelled after cutting the call.

SUNDAY

32

THE CAPTAIN'S STORY

We met Damodar at the tea-vendor's, and he paid the man to house us in his small accommodation for the night, which was half a kilometre down the road from his stall. His wife was a good hostess and had cooked a meal for us. The couple had two rooms, and after they had retreated to their bedroom, the three of us had the outside room to ourselves for the night. It wasn't luxurious, but was heaven compared to being on the road.

Everything had gone wrong, and we needed some time to take stock of the situation and plan our next move.

We chalked out alternative routes on a map, trying to figure out the best way to avoid Udhham Kumar and his teams. We knew he'd spread out his men and try to cover as much area as possible, in all directions. If Keshav and Shyam were a sign of what the rest of Udhham's teams was like, we were indeed in trouble. Hindsight is 20/20. Most people could read an optician's Snellen chart in reverse. If you knew the outcome, you wouldn't ever take a wrong decision. Why would you?

But having to take decisions based on incomplete information and changing circumstances, always made things different. Throw in hostility and more adversaries than you knew of, and believe me, half the world would withdraw into a shell, do nothing, and let time take the decision for them, even if that meant being caught in a burrow like we were.

Since the time Sylvia and I arrived at what one could call an idyllic location, only turmoil had been in our brains. Damodar had paid the vendor he had befriended.

We met Damodar at the tea-vendor's, and he paid the man to house us in his small accommodation for the night, which was half-a kilometre down the road from his stall. His wife was a good hostess and had cooked a meal for us. The couple had two rooms and after they had retreated to their bedroom, the three of us had the outside room to ourselves for the night. It wasn't the most luxurious, but was heaven compared to being on the road.

For some reason, what should have been a simple robbery and escape was terribly off kilter now. But it was what it was. Instead of whining and wasting precious time on what had gone wrong, we decided to focus on what to do next.

We chalked out alternative routes on a map, trying to figure out the best way to avoid Udhham Kumar and his teams. We knew he'd spread out his men and try to cover as much area as possible, in all directions. If Keshav and Shyam were a sign of what the rest of Udhham's teams were like, we were indeed in trouble. If those men and their sheer sizes weren't enough to frighten us, they were also armed.

Driving back to Delhi was out of the question. Bipin Patel wouldn't have forgotten us so soon.

But there were a few other options still open to us. Our main strategy focussed on getting off NH9 and taking some other route; we could go south towards Agra or Aligarh and then drive towards Kathmandu. Nepal shared its border with five Indian States and there were stretches where it wouldn't be impossible to slip in.

'You know Udhham best. What do you think he'll do now?' I asked Damodar.

'What do you mean?'

'We still don't know who that guy in the white Gypsy is; we don't even know if he's Udhham's man. As we said, we saw him back at Lajpat Nagar but we don't know if he's the one who discovered your new mobile number and called you. In any event, with or without him, Udhham would know two of his henchmen are dead and he'd know at least one of us is in the area.'

Both Sylvia and Damodar nodded, following my train of thought.

'So if you were Udhham, you'd also know we were on NH9, maybe hidden in the vicinity. So how would you trap us?'

'Udhham is very cunning. He'd have called in all his chips and there will be blockades everywhere we turn until we get out of UP – remember, he could use State Police. He'd be dead sure that we'll divert and I think we should double-bluff him, trust me—'

'You mean …' Sylvia looked befuddled, but I could see Damodar had a point.

'He's right, Sylvia. Udhham would be expecting us to go in all other possible directions expect the one we know he's on. There would be least traps and stops on the NH9.'

'He could leave some people behind on NH9…' Sylvia was reluctant.

'Not *could*, he certainly *would*, but he wouldn't put his maximum strength there. He'd send his best troops on other routes, that's what we're saying.'

'Hmm…'

We debated. Sylvia wasn't convinced at first, but Damodar and I managed to turn her in the end. I explained that in circumstances like these, it was best to stick to the plan and not make last minute modifications. If we believed that Udhham Kumar and/or Bipin Patel or anyone else had covered all surrounding roads, it made a lot of sense to take the shortest route.

'It's midnight now. Let's sleep until dawn and leave together in the same vehicle,' she said.

Damodar and I weren't inclined to travel together. So far, we'd succeeded in misdirecting our hunters by separating. And in any event, should one of us get trapped, the other team could still attempt to fight or flee. If we all got caught together, Udhham Kumar would be decorating our graves with poppy flowers before he peed on them.

Once again, I managed to convince Sylvia, though she still looked worried.

Our plan in place, we decided to get some shut eye. Sylvia and I took the floor, and Damodar used the cot our hosts had provided us with.

'Out of sheer curiosity, how long have you two known each other?' Damodar asked, lying on his bed.

'Very long,' I quipped. 'We're married.'

We were all up before daylight, much earlier than our hosts. Our trepidation was palpable. No one articulated it, but that leaden silence, ominously lingering in the room, expressed it all. The mood was grave. This wasn't a race for 200 million dollars anymore; it was a race for survival. If anyone – and at this moment, it felt like the whole world was looking for us – captured us, we'd be fortunate if we were executed painlessly.

Sylvia and I discarded some of our items; she put all her things, along with the painting, in my bag. We bid our hosts goodbye. Damodar gave them some money and took their SIM card, as his own number had been compromised and we had to stay in touch. It was time to leave.

Sylvia and I would travel in the Xylo we had nicked from the airport; Damodar would carry on in his Hyundai Accent. As far as we knew, the cars hadn't been compromised yet. Anyway, considering the location we were at, we didn't have the luxury of finding ourselves new wheels. We decided to take the city route, where I had spotted and tackled two of Udhham's men yesterday. I peeled off the blue stripes from my Xylo and changed the registration plates, just in case some passer-by had reported seeing our vehicle in the vicinity of the crime. I passed on one of the Chinese guns, which I had recovered from my loot last evening, to Damodar. We wished each other good luck and left – us following Damodar. I was at the wheel and Sylvia was in the back, ready with her Glock and H&K. I had my Glock 17 and the Chinese QSW semi-automatic, which I could use as a backup.

We didn't expect any roadblocks before we got on to the main road and we weren't disappointed. We turned right from our lane and picked up speed after we hit the highway. I could see Damodar looking in the rear-view mirror once in a while to confirm whether we were still following, him but he was very watchful of the surrounding landscape. He had to be. He was alone and it wasn't just the police roadblocks we were worried about – those were easy to spot from a distance – it was Udhham Kumar's or Bipin Patel's treacherous gang that would be harder to fight. They could be hiding anywhere; it would have been naïve to think that all of their men were as stupid as Shyam and Keshav, standing in the open to be sighted. The attack could be in any form from any side. Circa twenty kilometres later, the road bisected and as planned, we took the city route and Damodar veered right on to the Bypass.

In the distance, I could see chaos on the road where I had fought Shyam and Keshav the previous evening. The bodies had been removed but their car was still in place; there were two police vehicles sectioning off the area, which left only half the road for traffic to slowly pass. The police weren't stopping the vehicles, but they were making every effort to peep into decelerating vehicles like they expected the killer to return to the venue to admire his work. It was a potential hazard. If they saw Sylvia in the back, they might wonder why she wasn't in the front passenger seat with me. I told Sylvia to lie down on the rear bench seat and pretend to be unwell. We passed the point with no untoward incident.

We were to cross Hapur and carry on to the NH9. With Sylvia hidden out of sight, there was little chance that someone would recognise me as we drove past them. Both Sylvia and Damodar had cautioned me about not being reckless like I had been the evening before. What if the two goons I'd taken on yesterday had a back-up team that spotted me? So, even if I noticed a team skulking around the road or concealed in the bushes that I thought might be staking out for us, my orders were to carry on and not bother stopping. There was no point in inviting trouble – we needed to get out of the place as soon as we possibly could. I saw one such vigil before we got to Hapur and one within five kilometres of leaving the city; I might surely have missed some. What kind of manpower did these people have? I noticed that the stakeouts were now organised in teams of three; at least three people that I could spot. There could be more hidden from sight. I drove on.

33

As he drove on the bypass, Damodar's estimation was that it would be a sixteen- to twenty-kilometre run and then he'd join Sylvia and the Captain back on NH9. He decided to call them after a while to make sure everything was moving smoothly.

And that's when he noticed them. There was a large contingent camped at the petrol station on his right. And he was certain they had seen him too. Stopping to take a U-turn was out of question; they'd gun him down. His let his right hand gradually move down from the steering to pull out his Colt Python from the pocket in the door, but he never got the chance to aim or shoot. With his eyes focussed on the right side, he completely missed a red tractor that unexpectedly cut into the tarmac from the left. The Hyundai Accent went head on into the metal. The last thing he saw was the front end of his car crumbling.

The first team of men placed on the bypass had communicated to Udhham Kumar that Damodar was on the Hapur Bypass, headed in their direction. Udhham thanked them and told them not to follow him but to let him continue without any obstacles. He sent two teams across to the petrol station and asked the men he had borrowed from the local zamindar to park the tractor on the left of the tarmac. They were instructed to wait for a signal and then move the tractor on to the road to hit the Hyundai on the nearside. That would either wreck the car and bring it to an immediate halt or topple it, considering the mass of the tractor. Then he and his team would take over.

Damodar's car was now in sight and Udhham called the tractor driver and asked him to get ready and accelerate exactly when he instructed.

Either the tractor driver jumped the gun split seconds before or Udhham had underestimated the speed of the tractor. He saw the tractor cough hard as the driver accelerated and got it on to the tarmac before Damodar's Hyundai arrived at the spot, and instead of the heavy farm vehicle hitting the car as he had planned, it was the Hyundai, speeding over 100 kmph, that went headlong into the side of the tractor. The sound of metal on metal was deafening. The Hyundai's windshield was smashed into a million little pieces.

'Fucking idiot,' Udhham said as he saw SI Gupta rush to the car and followed him.

'He's dead,' declared the policeman, pulling his neck out of the window. The door had crumbled out of shape and jammed. 'Run.' He pointed towards the heavy black smoke coming out of the car's engine. The tractor driver had jumped off on the other side.

'Shit.' Udhham Kumar couldn't believe it. 'Shit, shit, shit,' he shouted.

The Hyundai burst into flame. Damodar was dead and cremated and Udhham was left none the wiser about the whereabouts of Sylvia or the Captain or his precious painting.

SI Hari Mohan Gupta tried to pull Udhham away from the tractor driver. The man had grabbed the driver's collar, and given him a resounding slap.

'It was an accident, Mr Kumar.' the policeman reasoned.

'Nonsense. I had asked him to jut in on time, but the bastard pulled the bloody tractor early, the buffoon. I'll shoot you!' he turned to the driver again.

'What? You asked him to hit Damodar's car?'

'Just a slight brush from the side. It was the best way to stop him, wasn't it? It was better than shooting at him.'

'That's not acceptable. You should have known it could kill him, and it did. Why didn't you tell me you were planning to do something like this when we've been talking about everything else since last night?'

'I didn't think you'd approve…'

'You're damn right I wouldn't approve. This is murder, Mr Kumar—'

'So be it. The bastard deserved to die. What are you going to do, charge me and arrest me? You're out of your jurisdiction and let me also tell you, you're out of your depth. Do you know who I am? What I can do to your career?'

'You're right. So I'm leaving. I can't be party to your illegal activities,' Hari Mohan said.

'Yes, leave. As if I called you here to help me. I deal with commissioners and not with *sub-inspectors*...'

Hari Mohan didn't wait to hear more. He turned around, got to his Gypsy and drove off. He must have driven just two hundred metres when he saw three jeep-loads of men arriving at the scene, and then he heard gunshots. Bipin Patel had arrived. He instinctively knew the two rogues would shoot first, talk later, and he doubted very much if either would survive. He pitied them but did not turn back. There was no way he was getting involved in the mess that was about to go down. Instead, he shifted the Gypsy into third gear and pushed the accelerator harder to get away from there as fast as he could.

34

THE CAPTAIN'S STORY

Udhham Kumar was tenacious, you had to give him that. He hadn't given up and we guessed he never would. The amount in question was a once-in-a-lifetime lottery; anyone in his position would have done exactly the same We'd known that and ergo, there wasn't any scope of being complacent. The more dangers we passed, the more we left behind. He couldn't have possibly hired the entire Indian Army to hunt us throughout the country. However many men he got, they would still be finite and the more distance we put between them and us, the safer we were. In theory, at least. Consequently, we drove to our destination without stopping unless absolutely necessary. We stopped once, after we were 200 kilometres out of Hapur, for Sylvia to hop out of the rear and sit in the front. We stopped at a small roadside dhaba on the outskirts of a village so small it wasn't even on the map, but it suited us. We had tea and left within five minutes. And we stopped for diesel once. We couldn't find a new vehicle on the way and we didn't see the need to change the car, but I did change the registration plates once. A Delhi registration number would unnecessarily stand out – should someone care to notice – in the rural heartland of Uttar Pradesh and Uttarakhand. And though there were other Delhi cars on the highway, it was safest to appear local.

We took the NH9 and not the State Highway 29. The landscape changed from dirty yellow to lush green as we moved into Uttarakhand. And our relief about getting out of UP made the pastures appear greener and lusher.

Sylvia tried calling Damodar at least half a dozen times on the new SIM he had acquired from the street vendor, but there was no response. Initially, the phone rang, but later, the calls began going straight to voicemail. Maybe the phone had run out of juice, or maybe it was out of range. Obviously, she didn't leave any messages. We were concerned, but not overly worried.

We finally reached Bhajanpur a few minutes after 7.30 p.m. Damodar had another twenty-four hours to get here.

'Where do we spend the night?'

'Let's find a hotel,' I said, but even after circling the place twice, we failed to find a place that wouldn't make us stand out like polar bears in a desert. If anyone came looking for us, we'd be caught out, irrespective of our guises.

'Why don't we go to the temple Damodar told us about and find a place nearby to park? We could maybe sleep in the jeep?' I suggested.

'Okay.'

I could easily transmogrify into my earlier monastic form, become a sanyasi again and sleep anywhere. The challenge this time was Sylvia, who – however plain you dressed her or made her look – could break God's meditation; anyone could figure out that we were not who we were pretending to be. And hence we dropped the idea. We parked the jeep about a kilometre away and walked to the temple to look-see the neighbourhood. The plan was to have dinner somewhere and return to our jeep for the night. Ideal for a hideaway – not totally invisible, but a parked vehicle isn't conspicuous either.

We found a local place near the temple and decided to eat there. Since we were its only customers, we were a bit exposed, no doubt, but it was better than being with the local crowd where a million eyes could see us. We wondered if Udhham Kumar or Bipin Patel had figured out that we had suckered them by our little trick at the Delhi Airport. But if they had taken the bait, how were Udhham and his men swarming in the vicinity of Hapur before us?

'Where is Damodar?' Sylvia looked concerned and rightly so. It had been quite some time since we had any contact. Almost ten hours now.

'I hope he ran out of battery and simply didn't bother to call because he's somewhere close, maybe just twenty-thirty kilometres away, and decided not to waste time stopping…'

'I don't have a good feeling about it.'

'Why?'

'I can't say, it's just a gut feeling…'

We paid the owner and walked out, hand in hand.

'I think we should call Damodar again,' Sylvia said. But before she could dial his number, her phone rang. 'It's

Damodar…' she exclaimed and pressed the green button to take the call. 'Hello, Damodar?'

'It's not Damodar, Sylvia …' The voice came from behind her, not from the phone.

We turned. A man dressed in a white short-sleeved shirt and khaki trousers stood about ten feet behind us. He was bald and in his mid-fifties – our anonymous stalker in the Gypsy.

'Who are you? And why do you have Damodar's phone?' she shot back.

'Sub-inspector Hari Mohan Gupta, Delhi Police.' He waved his ID at us, which in the dim light could have been his liquor permit for all we knew. But his gait, his demeanour, his mannerisms, all suggested he was a police officer, no doubt.

'What can we do for you, inspector?' I asked, stepping in front of Sylvia.

'Vagh Pratap Singh, I came all the way to arrest you … and don't bother reaching into your bag for any guns.' He pulled out his gun and aimed it at me.

We had packed our weapons, along with the painting, in the bag, which I slung on my shoulder when we had stepped out of the car. We didn't see any point in carrying the guns on us in this town, or into the temple. But we had been outfoxed. How much dumber could we be? We had managed to run over 700 kilometres only to be nabbed at the border, so close to the finish line.

'Where's Damodar?' Sylvia asked again.

'He's dead.'

'What? How? How do you know?' she exclaimed.

'Because I saw him die.'

'You killed him?'

'Of course not, I'm a police officer, not a criminal like you two.'

We stood motionless as the ramifications of what the policeman had just said sunk in. Damodar was dead.

But what if this guy was lying? It could be a trap.

'Well said, Inspector Gupta, but don't you think you are out of your jurisdiction?'

'So be it, but if you try to run, I'll still shoot.'

'How did Damodar die?' Sylvia pressed.

'Udhham Kumar got him killed.'

Sylvia sighed. 'No.'

'I saw it.'

'How did he get him killed?'

SI Gupta told us about a tractor and how Damodar crashed into it at high speed and died on the spot. 'In a way, it was a painless death, much less gruesome than if Udhham had caught him alive, trust me.'

'Why did that bastard have to kill Damodar?'

'That's why they say that you should think twice before you pull the pin out of the grenade. Once the pin is pulled out, it's done and you have to face the consequences.'

'How did you find us?' Sylvia asked.

He just raised Damodar's phone. 'I was first to reach Damodar when his car hit the tractor. I saw the phone and slipped it into my pocket without anyone noticing. The rest was easy.'

'Okay, inspector,' I said. 'Enough chatting. What do you want? No one comes alone to something like this, so where is your back-up?'

'I'm on my own. Captain, I thought arresting you and bringing you to justice would be my swan song. I didn't come after you only because of the painting. I've been looking for you ever since you escaped my colleagues after stealing and transporting weapons from the police armoury.'

'I didn't steal them—'

'Whatever. Transporting stolen goods, when you had knowledge of the fact that they were stolen, still qualifies as a crime.'

'What's the issue then? You have a gun in your hand, I don't. Arrest me.'

'That's the dilemma. The Van Gogh painting that Udhham told me about does not belong to any of you and if I arrest you, it would go back to some other crook, exactly like you or Bipin Patel. Besides, the people you've stolen it from are hardly the kind who'd sit and watch your trial. They are the vicious sort, who wouldn't think twice before killing both of you, even after they got the painting in their possession. But you already know that, don't you?'

We nodded.

'If I arrest you and take you back, I don't think you'll get justice. I've seen it happen so many times that I've lost faith in our system. The people you've stolen from this time around are extremely influential. They'll bend every rule that I've tried to uphold all my life. If they cannot kill you in cold blood, they'll get you killed by corrupt officials.'

I didn't understand this man. If he didn't want to arrest us, why had he come all the way? To give me a lecture?

'Good then. Let's all shake hands and go our own way. Thank you for stopping by, Inspector,' I said, sticking my hand out.

'Not so fast. I'm here to warn you *and* advise you.'

'So from a hunter, you've turned into our messiah?'

He shook his head. We were out of the temple boundary and there was an incandescent light bulb on, some fifteen feet from us, five feet behind the Inspector, and light illuminated the gun he was holding. And if it was fully loaded –we had no reason to believe otherwise – it had seventeen rounds. Even if Sylvia and I sprinted, there was a very high probability that at least one of us would be shot, most likely fatally. He was a trained policeman, not an amateur. The truth was that we had let the guard down and now we'd have to pay the price.

'Okay, so what's your advice? What should we do now?' I asked.

'A simple deal, an exchange offer, as some might say.'

'Go on, let's hear it.'

'You hand over the painting to me and I'll help you cross the border into Nepal. You'll be safe once you cross into Nepal. It's that simple.'

'So greed's takes over after all? After all that spiel about us being crooks …? I thought you said you were an upright policeman who believed in justice. What happened suddenly? 200 million dollars proved too much for your conscience, Inspector Gupta? And what, we give this painting to you and you expect us to work as farm labourers in Nepal for the rest of our lives?'

'I cannot help you with your career choices, Captain. That'll be your decision.'

'Give it to him,' Sylvia said before I could respond. I looked at her open-mouthed. Was she serious? Had we taken all this risk to meekly surrender the painting to this man?

'No blooming way.' I was furious. 'Let me make you a counter offer, Inspector … why don't we sell the damn thing and share the proceeds? Now isn't that a win-win proposition?'

'That's another charge I can book you for, you know? An attempt to bribe an officer of the law.'

'So let me get this straight. If you get the painting, you sell it back to Udhham Kumar or Bipin Patel or whoever, and you pocket the money, but you are not agreeable to sharing the booty with us. I like your style – it's all or nothing for you. Is that just because you're the one holding a gun?'

'You got me wrong. I won't be selling this painting or returning it to any of those crooks. I will not even take it back to the police station since I know it will be returned to Bipin Patel. I will take it to the highest authority in India and ensure that it is returned to the museum it was pinched from. This is an international treasure, it belongs to some museum. It is meant to be displayed, not rolled and kept hidden away in someone's personal collection.'

'I like the way you think, inspector, but you and I both know that that's never going to happen. Whoever you hand it over to will sell it again and make mega-millions and you'd think you've done right.'

'As I said, it's your choice, Captain, but you don't have the luxury of time to make it. Udhham Kumar and Bipin Patel are coming after you. So what will it be – the painting or your lives? Or I can take you back to jail and I still get the painting, whether you like it or not.'

'Why are you doing this?' I was genuinely curious.

'Let's give him the painting and get away from here,' Sylvia said.

'See, the lady has more sense than you. Forget this painting, cross over to Nepal and be free. Or you will rot in some jail for the rest of your life for the double-homicide of Udhham Kumar's men.'

'I didn't kill both, I only shot one, and that too, in self-defence.'

'It will be your word against mine, and who knows what the judge will decide, given your criminal history. You want to take that chance?'

I have been a criminal. But I hadn't killed anyone before. Even if I had a gun at this moment, I doubt whether I'd be able to shoot the Inspector and kill him in cold blood. Stealing, robbing, lock-picking, transporting stolen goods – those were the highest points in my crime chart. It seemed like we had reached a point of no return. The Inspector was right – we'd be killed or locked up for the rest of our lives. And who knew, Nepal would have other opportunities if we survived.

'How do we know you'd take us across the border if we give the painting to you?'

'You don't, but you have to trust me. What other choice do you have?'

I decided to go for it. I moved my hand to unzip the bag, thinking that maybe, just maybe, I'd be able to surreptitiously pull out the gun under the pretext of taking out the painting, but—

'Not so fast, Captain. Don't open that bag. I know you have guns in it. Sylvia, I want you to take the bag from your partner's shoulder and, without attempting to play any tricks, bring it to me.'

I stood still as Sylvia took the bag and walked towards the inspector. Our last chance was slipping away. The nearer Sylvia got to him, the further away our plan got from us.

'Now,' he said, when Sylvia was two feet away from him. 'Unzip the bag slowly so I can see your hands, and take the painting out.'

Sylvia took out the tube – the two-hundred-flipping-million-dollar tube that had cost Damodar his life. I hadn't been acquainted with him for long, but in the little time I had known him, he was just another of my kind who had somehow slipped onto the wrong side of the tracks due to destiny or circumstance, and never found anyone to pull him back. He wasn't a malicious bastard like Udhham Kumar. How would we face his mother now? Would we even go to see her? A thousand thoughts swam in my mind. In the background, I saw the Inspector asking Sylvia to hand over the guns to him too.

I saw him make Sylvia take out the painting, unfold it and show it to him before rolling it and putting it back in the tube.

'Thank you. Move back, please,' the inspector said, taking the painting from her.

Sylvia walked back with the bag that now only carried an assortment of disguises as well as a few fake car registration plates.

'I'm sorry,' I murmured as I hugged Sylvia when she came close.

'We were in it together, remember, Captain? And we are alive and free. Let's take it a day at a time. Don't lose hope.'

'How do we cross the border now?' I asked.

'You come with me in my vehicle.'

'It's a white Gypsy, isn't it?' He was indeed the bald guy we had first spotted at Lajpat Nagar and assumed was working for Udhham Kumar. It was a big mistake to have overlooked him, but there were so many people hunting for us, it had been impossible to keep track.

'Yes. Do you need anything from your jeep?'

'You mean, we have to leave our vehicle behind?'

'Yes.'

'How do we travel ahead then, after you drop us at the border?'

'Guys, I promised to help you cross the border, and I will keep my word. I didn't say I'd run a taxi service for you, did I?'

SI Gupta took all precautions. He handcuffed both of us and made us sit in the rear and drove to the border. On the way, he told us that he had kept some news from us; that he had seen the gunfight begin at Hapur Bypass and had later been informed by his sources that the total body count had been over twenty, but that the corpses hadn't been identified yet. For all we knew, Udhham Kumar and Bipin Patel were dead.

'So there was no threat from them if we had returned?' I shouted. 'You lied to us!'

'No, as I mentioned, I just held back something. Plus, we don't know if either or both of them survived. And don't forget, you are still wanted by the Delhi police.'

At the border, he locked the vehicle, got down, spoke to the people and, after five minutes, we were on our way.

Bhimdatta was roughly ten kilometres from the border. He stopped the car near a waiting bus that was bound for a place called Nepalgunj, uncuffed us, said bye and turned around to return. We knew Kathmandu was about 200 kilometres away and the bus leaving for Nepalgunj was going in the right direction. With limited choice at 11 p.m., we boarded the near-empty bus and dozed off immediately, even before it left Bhimdatta, only to wake up in the morning when the bus had arrived at its destination, at 6 a. m.

MONDAY

35

THE CAPTAIN'S STORY

The first thing we did was to throw away our phones and get new ones. We decided against carrying on to Kathmandu in public transport. In case a Nepalese law enforcement officer stopped us, we'd face problems as we had no papers on us. The last thing either of us wanted after coming this far was detention or deportment. Thus, we resorted to what I did best – we nicked a car. There was a local station with a sea of unattended parked cars. I wasn't comfortable using one of the fake Indian registration plates we were carrying and hence, after we identified a SsangYong Kyron that appeared to be a four-wheel drive, I unscrewed the registration plates and switched them with a similar looking SsangYong, and we were on our way to Kathmandu.

I drove and let Sylvia rest. It was still a good 600 kilometres away. I drove in silence, a feeling of overwhelming remorse and regret enveloping me. I felt guilty about letting Damodar go on his own, but if we were with him at the time, we'd have met the same fate.

'Shouldn't we go to Siddhartanagar to see Damodar's mother?' I asked when Sylvia woke up. 'I see no sense in going to Kathmandu first. We need to get some proper documents...'

'No, we should go to Kathmandu first,' Sylvia insisted.

'What's the point—'

'What if I told you I have another job lined up for us?'

'I'd say you're kidding me!' I looked at her and she looked back, her face serious. 'When did you set it up?'

'Captain, sometimes the mentee turns out to be smarter than the mentor.'

'Oh, I completely agree,' I admitted. 'But what's the job?'

'I'll tell you when we get there.'

We stopped at 2 p.m., had some coffee and sandwiches, got some packed and then recommenced our journey with Sylvia at the wheel.

We switched places again before we arrived in Kathmandu at 9 p.m. Sylvia was on the phone to get us a sumptuous suite in Dwarika's Hotel, and it took us twenty minutes to negotiate and find our way to Battisputli, where the grand hotel was.

The staff at the hotel was very helpful and obliging, and our driving licences were enough as ID proof.

'Aren't you forgetting something, Captain?' she asked when we got to our rooms and I lay down on the bed, exhausted.

I racked my tired brain to think of something I may have missed. 'No.'

'Are you sure?'

'I'm sorry, but I'm knackered. I can't remember anything, Sylvia.'

'Do you remember how to make love?'

I smiled.

'That I do.'

TUESDAY

36

THE CAPTAIN'S STORY

I woke up at midnight and heard someone murmuring. I switched on my night-light to see that Sylvia was not in bed. I realised the whispers were coming from the front room in our suite. She was talking to someone. Then I heard the suite door open and slam shut. Someone just left our suite. I got up, put on my robe and rushed to the front room where Sylvia stood next to the dining table, her back to me.

'Who was that, Sylvia?'

'Who?'

'Who just left the suite?'

She turned and with a pull of her hand, tied her robe tighter. 'There was no one here.'

'I heard voices. There was definitely someone in this room.'

'Are you doubting me, Captain?'

'No.'

Then she moved aside and I saw it. There was a chocolate cake on the table and her words from last night flashed in my mind. *'Aren't you forgetting something, Captain?'*

Of course, it was my birthday! She had arranged for a cake for me in the middle of the night, despite the fact that she was equally tired and had been through the same hell as me over the last few days. 'Happy birthday, my love,' she said and smiled, moving forward. She wrapped her arms around me and kissed me. We embraced, and suddenly, I felt something like a long and thick gun nozzle press against my right thigh.

I withdrew immediately. 'What's that?'

'Why don't you find out yourself?' she said, and stuck a leg out of the robe.

I unknotted the sash of her robe and in one swift motion, pulled it off her. There, along her long, gorgeous leg, I saw a tube taped to her upper thigh.

'Your birthday gift, Captain. From me to you. Gurudakshina. Be careful, it is worth Two. Hundred. Million. Dollars.'

I carefully removed the tube, opened it and pulled the rolled-up painting out. I unfolded it on the dining table next to my birthday cake.

It was the *Poppy Flowers.*

'How did you...?' That was all I could manage to ask, my voice soft with disbelief.

'Remember I had gone to Mumbai for two days while you were romancing Sheena?'

'Not romancing Sheena, but yes I remember your trip...'

'I didn't tell you *why* I was off to Mumbai. I'd told Udhham Kumar that I was visiting my church. That wasn't a complete lie...'

She opened a packet kept beside the cake and pulled out the candles. As she arranged them on the cake, she told me that most people thought of Bollywood when they thought of Mumbai, or saw it as the financial hub of the country. They forgot that the city was full of history more colourful than most other places – the art, the culture, the diversity, and not to forget, the churches. There were over a hundred and twenty Roman Catholic churches in Mumbai. And they had been built largely under the patronage of Portuguese missionaries. And that was why she had gone to Mumbai.

As we cut the cake, fed pieces to each other and kissed, she educated me about some of the older churches in Mumbai that were built as early as the sixteenth century. Many of them had been rebuilt, renovated, redecorated, and a few of them carried old paintings – some from the time of their inception, and others, that were more recent, replacing the older ones. She had gone looking for a painting that had been replaced in the mid- to late-nineteenth century, and was from that era – Van Gogh's era. She had also done her research, she told me, and found that most painters of Van Gogh's era used a plain-weave canvas.

'Thankfully, Mr Van Gogh didn't deviate too often. He generally used the typical finely woven portrait linen like most others since it was believed that finely woven linen absorbed oil quicker and retained a better finish.

'I didn't care what was painted on it as long as the canvas was of the period, and it was bigger than twenty-six by twenty-one inches. I knew the work on the canvas could be erased by denatured alcohol. It would leave a foul smell, but I had the time to let the odour die.'

'So you just walked into a church and took the painting?'

'It wasn't that simple. It took me the best part of a day to visit eight Catholic churches in Bandra and Khar and to identify three churches that carried older paintings on the walls, in sizes bigger than the one I needed, and shortlist the one I thought would be easiest to get access to. Then I went shopping for the tools I needed. I returned in time only to attend evening mass on weekdays at 7.30 p.m. and made a note of the possible entrances.

'Then, suddenly, for some strange reason, I began to feel bad about breaking into God's house. So I changed tack and scouted for a nook to disappear into for a few hours. When the mass ended and the congregation rambled out, I took the opportunity to move sideways unnoticed and hid in the nook, only to come out once I was sure that everyone, including the pastors, had left. The main lights had been switched off; only the twinkling ones near the statues were on.' She stopped to have another bite of cake.

'What happened then?'

'There were a few choices. I decided to go for the ones farthest from the altar. But as I moved towards the rear end of the pews, I noticed that the tower of the church, where the access to the bell was, had a small area that seemed stocked with something that had old bedsheets thrown over. I turned, looked for the stairs and climbed up. From a distance, I could see that whatever was under the sheets had been there for months, possibly years. The dust was a few millimetres thick and untouched. And beneath it lay exactly what I was searching for – a huge stock of old paintings, statues, and other things that had been thrown aside to give way to the new. I picked the ones I needed, took out my knife, cut the frame open, took the canvas, put the bed sheet back, and silently slipped out of the church after midnight.'

'And you took one?'

'I took two canvases, just in case; the second one a kind of insurance, in case the painter went horribly wrong and ruined the first canvas, I returned to Delhi, erased them and put them in a bedroom to dry and lose the lingering whiff of ethanol. Then I found a local artist and got him to paint a replica of *Poppy Flowers* on the canvas. He was good. I knew the fake could fool anyone because of the age of the canvas, and it did.'

'Wait till Sub-inspector Hari Mohan Gupta finds out.'

'It'll be too late by then.'

'But when did you switch the two paintings?'

'I wasn't sure about Damodar in the beginning, so back at the hotel at Barakhamba Road, I placed the fake under the car seat and kept the original in my bag. Later, when we rearranged all our stuff into a single bag, I wrapped the original in my clothes and slipped it at the bottom, and kept the fake on top. Quite frankly, I was a little frightened when the Inspector wanted me to show him all the contents so he could check for weapons, so instead, I gave him all that we had and kept the painting under wraps. It worked.'

We kissed again. I didn't know whether I wanted to laugh or cry with pride and relief. 'You are a genius, Sylvia.'

'You taught me everything I know, Captain. We are a team.'

'How do we sell this now?' I looked at the painting on the table.

'Mr Haruhiko Sakai is arriving in Kathmandu tomorrow afternoon. He'll see us in the casino at 9.30 p.m.'

'And I thought I was the smart conman.'

'Don't beat yourself up.' She winked. 'I couldn't have done any of this alone. I would have given up the search for the painting in the first two weeks. Now, let's sleep, we need to go shopping in the morning.'

I looked at her quizzically.

'What, you want to go to a casino for a multi-million-dollar deal in the same stinking old jeans we've been wearing for the past few days?'

'Oh yes. Let's get this painting cashed and then go and see Damodar's mother.'

'Are you feeling nervous by any chance, Captain?' Sylvia asked. We were sitting in The Dwarika's Fusion Bar. It was elegantly designed with a parquet floor and exposed brickwork. It overlooked the swimming pool, though at this hour, it was empty. There was a live band playing jazz – Dave Brubeck. I ordered a Macallan and she sipped a margarita. I looked at my girl. She looked gorgeous as always, in a short black cocktail dress that would do Coco Chanel proud.

'No, I'm not,' I replied to her question, albeit timidly, a little doubtful of myself for the first time in years. I had missed far too many things, which made me wonder if I was losing my touch.

'Mrs and Mr Singh?' asked the barman.

'Yes,' Sylvia responded.

'My Sakai has arrived, and he's waiting for you at the reception.'

'Thank you.'

We upended our drinks, signed the bill to the room and got up. Sylvia put her arm in mine and we walked up to the reception.

THE NEXT SIX MONTHS

37

THE CAPTAIN'S STORY

Our meeting with Mr Sakai, the Japanese art collector, had gone just as expected. His expert took an hour to establish the authenticity of the painting, but there was no way he could have paid us in Kathmandu. We needed time to establish identities in Nepal and to open bank accounts before he could transfer the funds. We had to keep the painting for another six months. For some strange reason, he trusted us despite knowing the circumstances in which the painting had been acquired, leaving corpses in its wake. At least he trusted us enough to give us a generous advance so we didn't look for a buyer elsewhere. Not that we had planned to double-deal on this occasion, but did he really think he'd take me to the International Court of Justice to claim entitlement to a stolen property?

We honeymooned in Kathmandu for a week after the meeting. Not keen to take any further risks, we hired a cab from Kathmandu to Siddhartanagar to meet Damodar's mother. Siddhartanagar was a small town with a population of 150,000 people.

Meeting Damodar's mother was a revelation. She was weak and appeared older than her sixty-two years that Damodar had mentioned. She seemed to have earned the wrinkles from the strains of indigent life. We wondered whether we should somehow sugar coat the harshness of the news but eventually decided it wouldn't be fair to lie. The news of her only child's death virtually destroyed her. Damodar had left Nepal about a decade back, and although there had been no communication between them, except the occasional phone call, she had nursed hope that he'd return. For several minutes after we revealed ourselves as his friends and told her he had died in an accident, there was no reaction. And then she fell in a dead faint. For a week after, she was in critical condition. The shock had been too much to bear. We decided to stay until she recovered.

One day, she finally got up from her bed and managed to walk over to where we were sitting. She sat down and took Sylvia's hands in her trembling ones.

'I'm sorry I was so consumed by my own loss, I didn't even ask you your names. And you came all the way to help me,' she said, holding Sylvia's hands in hers.

We told her our names, but she shook her head, smiling.

'You're like my own children now. I'll call you Damodar,' she told me, and …' she turned to Sylvia.

'I'll be Sonia,' Sylvia said, and that made me smile. It was the name we'd decided on – Damodar, Sylvia and I.

It was simple to open a bank account as Sonia Yadav and Damodar Yadav, but it was a small bank and the amount of money we were expecting would have raised suspicion. But one small account paved the way for us, and we opened a few more accounts in bigger banks in the next couple of months. Mr Sakai's trustworthy soldier arrived and the exchange took place smoothly.

We'd been there six months now. In the meantime, we got to know that both Udhham Kumar and Bipin Patel were dead, courtesy each other, just like the inspector had suspected. However hard we tried, it was impossible to shed a tear.

Sheena, my dedicated student and fan, might curse me for the rest of her life, but she was safe, now that Patel was gone.

We also found out that SI Hari Mohan Gupta retired, a good, steady servant of the Indian police service – nothing more or less.

So as a matter of fact, nothing was stopping us from returning to India. We could easily move back and live in luxury. Our original plan had been to stay here until we received the money, gave Damodar's mother what we had promised, or even more if she asked for it, arranged new passports and left for the Caribbean or some other place that would accept us as residents. We had enough money to buy citizenship in any country we wanted.

Damodar's mother declined all offers of money, no matter how hard we pleaded, leaving us with far too much money and far too little to do with it. But her bond with us was growing stronger, and I was afraid she'd die if we left her.

'What's our plan?' Sylvia asked one night as we slept on the roof terrace, the stars shining down on us from a clear sky.

'I don't know. I didn't realise winning could be as boring as losing. To be honest, I'm the happiest I've been since my parents died, and it's not because of the money we've made—'

'I know. I was thinking the same. I'm pregnant, Captain.'

'Really?'

'Yes, isn't that amazing?'

'When did you come to know?'

'Just this morning.'

'Have you told Ma?'

'Yes, I have.'

We looked into each other's eyes; our subliminal affection for Ma and joy at getting the second childhood that we had both missed first time around was palpable.

They say, sometimes, just one single moment defines your life.

That instant, that one moment summed it all up for us.

I bought enough land to start a co-operative dairy farm to employ families in the neighbourhood; Sylvia adopted the local school and orphanage. We had come here as fugitives, looking to organise fake IDs and sort out paperwork to fly away to somewhere exotic and expensive. It took us half a year to realise we had already been at the somewhere we'd been looking for our entire lives. We finally had what we could call home, and there was no need to run anymore.

AUTHOR'S NOTE

Vincent van Gogh's Poppy Flowers is one of his only paintings that has been stolen twice, as mentioned in the story.

The market price of the painting is indeterminable. It depends on a lot of variables – who owns it, what condition it is in now, who the buyer is or how many private collectors are seeking it. Various websites and experts have attempted at valuing it based on the last work of Van Gogh legitimately sold, drawing comparisons with other paintings of the same era, building statistical models after indexing for inflation... Honestly speaking, no one could possibly give an exact figure until the piece is returned to experts to evaluate. After going through multiple sources I decided to put the value of the painting as USD 200 million. If nothing else, it was a nice round figure.

Quite frankly, irrespective of what the actual value of Van Gogh's Poppy Flowers is today – USD 100 million or 200 – it takes away nothing from the story.

As it's whereabouts weren't known when I penned this story, I took the liberty to fictionalise that the said piece of art was somewhere in India. If it were ever found, no one would be able to establish all the unsavoury hands it exchanged since it's theft in 2010 until its recovery and hence, the fact/fiction that it was briefly in India doesn't take away anything from this book. I could have just as easily fictionalised the name of the artist and a lost painting of certain value, but why pick fiction when truth sounds far more interesting?

This book wouldn't have been completed without Nidhi, my wife and partner in crime. It certainly wouldn't have been in the shape it is in if it weren't for my literary agent, Siyahi. And it wouldn't be in your hands if it weren't for my publishers, HarperCollins India. Lastly, there would be no sense in writing if it were not for you, lovely readers. I sincerely thank all the wonderful people mentioned above for helping me grow as a writer and as a human being. I hope you like *The Heist Artist.*

Love, lots of it.

Vish Dhamija

Find me on: Facebook: www.facebook.com/vishdhamija
Twitter: @vishdhamija
Email: vishdhamija@gmail.co